William Newton

The morning Star or Way-Side Musings and Other Poems

William Newton

The morning Star or Way-Side Musings and Other Poems

ISBN/EAN: 9783744764407

Printed in Europe, USA, Canada, Australia, Japan

Cover: Foto ©Andreas Hilbeck / pixelio.de

More available books at **www.hansebooks.com**

THE MORNING STAR;

OR,

WAY-SIDE MUSINGS,

AND

Other Poems.

BY

WILLIAM NEWTON,

RECTOR OF THE CHURCH OF THE NATIVITY, PHILADELPHIA.

PHILADELPHIA:
CLAXTON, REMSEN & HAFFELFINGER,
624, 626 & 628 MARKET STREET.
1874.

T HE story of this Little Book is very soon told.
Twenty - five years ago, the subject first sug-
gested itself. The course of thought, in its general
outline, was determined on; the title selected, and the
opening lines, as they now stand, were written. It was
to be, literally, *Way-Side Musings;* for those lines were
written — as, indeed, I expected the whole to be —
during the course of my daily walk of three miles, to
and from the school I was then teaching. How well
do I remember turning aside, and resting my little
blank book on the top-rail of the worm-fence, by the
road-side, as I hurriedly dotted down my thoughts.

I was younger then than now: and supposed that I
could finish my Poem, before my six months' engage-
ment as a Teacher, had expired. But I retain the Title
still; for I confess to a fondness for it which it would
be false to deny, and foolish to attempt to conceal.

Since that time, this subject has never been forgotten : and my purpose concerning it, never laid aside. Consciously and unconsciously, my thoughts have dwelt upon it. Its completion has been the purpose of my life. It is my Life Thought. More than anything else, I have desired to put into form, the conceptions of the Love of God, manifested in Jesus Christ, as they move and glow in my own heart. Perhaps they may cheer and strengthen others, as they have cheered and strengthened me. Still, I lay down my pen, with a sort of regret, as I remember that *Way-Side Musings* and I, are to be travelling companions no more!

PHILADELPHIA, October, 1873.

CONTENTS

THE MORNING STAR.

CANTO I.

MISCELLANEOUS POEMS.

CANTO FIRST.

GOD'S GREAT DESIGN.

xi

CANTO I.

ARGUMENT: Invocation: Design everywhere, manifest. Why? End of Art not its own display; Something beyond. So God has a great end in view. Greatness of, inferred from Creation's greatness. Creation, what? Revelations of Astronomy. God before them all. Saw all He meant to do; and all that would come of His doing it. Saw it was best to do it. Evils of Sin. Redemption. God's Plan for putting them all away: and bringing in greater blessings. Redemption, no after-thought. First in order with Him. Creation a consequence of Redemption.

Eternity of God. Always the same. But who tell us this? God must reveal Himself. The World, a stage for this. How made? Creation; what we learn from? Difficulties in. Cannot remove them. Must wait. For what? God manifest in Christ. Result of His work. His Cross, Central Figure in the Universe. God displayed therein. Earth, as having borne the Cross: What it shall be? Full history of, not yet reached. All ills removed by Redemption. God's Self-Revelation, His great end: Would have all His creatures know and love Him. Therefore, reveals Himself: General summing up.

THE MORNING STAR.

GOD'S GREAT DESIGN.

I.

ETERNAL Spirit! Source of Light and Truth!
With whom no darkness dwelleth! In whose sight,
The things that are, and those that shall be, lie
Alike disclosed, both as to secret cause
And unknown consequence: to Thee I come,
And ask for light to guide me. Hold my hand
That I may stumble not, nor go astray.
Within my spirit shine to give the light
Of Thine own Spirit. Teach me how to soar
Up to the height of Thine own thought, and trace
Its grand unfolding, as it always dwelt,
A living fact with Thee. For who can think
Thought so adventurous by himself, alone?
Drive Thou away my darkness. On my sight,
Pour Thy celestial ray. Let all within

Be instinct with Thyself: that I may show
Thine own conceptions to the sons of men.

II.

The world is full of infinite design.
There's not an atom in the boundless range
Of Nature's vast dominions, but sustains
Its wise relations; works some given end;
And yields obedience to its special law.
And Science, in the grandeur of its march,
Now, through the wonders of the starry worlds;
And now, through those the Microscope reveals;
And all that lie between, teaches this truth,
That nothing is, but for some higher end
Than its own being.   Every thing that is,
Works for some other thing; and serves, through
        that,
A purpose nobler than itself alone
Could reach in the Great Plan. The autumn leaf
Falls not without its mission; and the breeze,
That scarcely sways the willow's pendent bough,
Has its own law; and serves its end as well,
As do the rise and setting of the sun.
The dew-drop's brightness is not for itself:
The floweret's beauty has not been in vain,
When Man beholds it not: for everywhere,
The law of uses is the law of God.
And all His works proclaim one Ruling Mind,
And take their place in some exact design.

III.

Can we unfold the reason ?   Can we tell
Why this display of Wisdom and of Power?
Can we, without presumption, seek to lift
The veil that hides His purpose from our view?
This much, at least, is clear.   Not for itself
Was Earth called into being.   There must be
Some purpose, higher than the mere display
Of Infinite perfections; or this world
And its surrounding orbs would ne'er have been.
Suns, Stars and Flowers alike proclaim this truth;
And speak of something as the Primal Thought,
In the Creator's mind.   E'en human Art
Keeps this before it; and in all its works
Proposes to itself some worthier end,
Than the display of art.   Is it for this
Our Steamers plough the Ocean?   Is it this
That bids our Railroads stretch their iron bands
Across the continent, and into one
United Whole bind all its differing parts?
Is it for this that Telegraphic wires
Circle the globe; and at each hearth-stone, tell
The daily news from earth's remotest bounds?
Man's Art can do all this; but in it all,
Acts for some fitting end.   It looks beyond ;
And to the purpose, it designs to serve,
Adapts the means it uses.   And shall we
Interpret our Creator, by a rule

Unworthy of ourselves? Shall we believe,
That when He manifests creative skill,
And bids the Universe display His power,
He has no thought beyond its mere display?
No. From Creation's grandeur, we infer
How infinitely glorious must be
The Great Design for which the World was made:
The mighty Plan for whose development,
He forms a sphere, magnificent as this!

IV.

But who can tell how vast Creation is?
We take the glass of the Astronomer,
And turn it to the sky. What meets our gaze?
See! From the far-off worlds that roll above;
From other Suns and Systems, beams of light,
On their long journey of uncounted years,*
Come thronging to the eye! What are those beams?
News-Bearers from those shining orbs; and bring
Tidings from distant worlds—perhaps from worlds,
No longer in existence. Who can tell?
Who can declare what changes may have swept
Across their surface, since to this, our Earth,
Those beams of light set forth? Or could we stand,
As sentinels, upon the outside world,
Of this our little System ; and look out

* "The rays of light from the remotest nebulæ must have been about two millions of years on their way." — *Sir Wm. Herschell, in Transactions for* 1802, p. 498.

Into the space beyond; what would we see?
Myriads of worlds, in strange profusion cast —
Star-clouds, compacted in such close array,
That, to our vision, they appear as belts
Of milky light, which no resolving power
Of Telescope can separate. Yet each
Has its own orbit; and moves calmly forth ·
In its appointed time. Outside of these,
Others are seen; lying as far from them,
As these are from our System; and yet, all
Form one harmonious and united whole.
And Thought is dumb, and Fancy droops its wings,
Before this grand display of worlds on worlds,·
As countless as the drops of morning dew!
Yet, in Creation's System, ere the first
Of those innumerable orbs had birth;
Ere in the silence of eternity,
Creation's work first sounded, — God was there;
As, through the unbroken silence of the past,
He had forever, been. The Cause, uncaused;
Standing before all being; in Himself
The Source and Origin of all beside.
For God's *I Am* becomes the active source
Of everything that is. Apart from Him,
There is no life, no motion. He contains
The spring of all things in Himself alone.
And, as He wills it, they go forth, and are
The countless forms of life and joy that make
The glorious fulness of Creation's works.

2 *   B

V.

Alone, in His eternity He saw
All that He meant to do.   Before His glance
There rose the perfect vision of His works.
As first He formed them; and as once again
. They shall appear, when the restraining power
Of Sin shall be no more; and Earth shall wear
The sinless glory of her first estate.
He saw it all; and, as it stood defined
In His conception of the blessedness
That would result therefrom, His Spirit owned
The sense of joy, that joy imparted, gives.
For, all the blessings that would surely flow
From His great work, would be secured alone
By His Self-Sacrifice.   Yet, seeing this,
All His delights were with the sons of men;
And with the outcome of that glorious plan,
That measured His own fulness in the Cross.
'T was not Creation only that inspired;
But, in its budding glories, He beheld
The fruits of full Redemption,   And for this,
He measured out the universe; and breathed
The living spirit of a thought of God
Through all His works; and to its music, set
Alike the least and loftiest of His works.
Nothing escaped His glance.   Each special act
That swells Creation's history; each world
That was to be created; every form,

Which, in the cycle of revolving years,
He destined to inhabit it, He saw;
And, in the fulness of His searching glance,
Gave each its place and mission.   Every change
That was to sweep its surface; every law
That governed every portion, and impressed
Their properties on matter's countless forms
Each act of each of its inhabitants;
And the vast total of results that flow
As one begets another, and links in
To form causation's never-ending chain;
Rose up before Him, as His eye surveyed
What He designed to do.   It stood defined,
As the Creator's Panoramic view,
Revolving silently before His glance,
Ere His great work began.   For in His mind,
That always *is*, which He designs to do.
He is its being.   It exists in Him.
Heaven is the open page on which He writes;
And worlds flow forth as words do from the pen
With which we trace our thoughts.   But, ere His
        hand
Had written out those glorious characters
That make Creation's beauty, they were still
Facts in His purpose; no less fixed and sure
Than when He gave to them objective form
Before His creatures' vision.   In His mind,
They were, because He willed them; but to us,
They come, as stars do, living in the light,

Yet looking down upon us from the sky,
Only when darkness brings them out to view.

VI.

And thus, in perfect range, His eye took in
His Great Design, and every consequence
Near and remote, that would result therefrom.
All the disturbing causes that would spring
From Man's revolt; and the unending ills
That would have spread, like ripples on the lake,
Until they reached Creation's utmost bound;
If it were left unmatched and unatoned,
Came into view before Him.   It was not
An unforeseen event, when Man resolved
To set up his own will against the will
Of his Creator, as his rightful law;
And try the Evil, as a thing unknown,
And so, by possibility, a Good.
No.   Its occurrence was a thing assumed,
As the dark background of the glorious Plan,
By which all evil shall be put away:
The Problem of Creation solved, at last;
The good secured; and every creature fixed
In loving loyalty before His throne.
And in the Coming Day, when this Great Thought
Of the Creator, statue-like, shall be
Unveiled before His creatures: they shall see
Its grand results achieved: the world redeemed;

And men and angels made to stand secure,
In the great issues of the work of Christ.
Self-Revelation therefore is the end
He always had in view; since thus alone,
He could attract all creatures to Himself;
And thus enable them to find in Him,
The Source and Secret of all creature good!
God, rightly known is God supremely loved.

VII.

This was the vision that before Him rose;
And seeing it, He still, esteemed it best,
To give Creation scope; and thus bring in
Redemption's glorious scheme; which underlies
All else that God has done.   For all His works
Are but as Heralds in forerunning this.
Creation was determined on, because
Redemption was His purpose.   And the worlds
That Science has revealed; or, with the aid
Of stronger instruments may, yet, make known;
Are only points, in which the full display
Of God's Great Purpose in the work of Christ,
Shall yet, be fully made.   It shall be known
Throughout Creation's limits.   Everywhere,
The story of His love shall be rehearsed,
By those who know its fulness; and the worlds
Now, only known as distant stars, shall be
Prepared as Homes where His redeemed shall
      dwell.

In gushing sweetness, through the fields of light,
The story of Redemption, through His blood,
Shall yet be heard for everlasting years,
And every star be vocal with His praise.
Creation finds its meaning in the Cross.
Its real grandeur awes you and inspires
As there you trace God's thoughts; and see the
      work
That complements Creation, take its place,
Beaming serenest light, and filling it,
Not with the glory of a God of Power,
So much as with the wonders of His Love.

VIII.

God, then, existed from eternity,
The same that He is now.   The same in love:
In His capacity for love the same:
The same in everything that makes Him God.
Yet who shall know this?   Who shall make it
      known;
Or show to Man the mystery of God?
Only Himself.   The Finite cannot soar
To grasp the Infinite; and Man would be
Equal to God, if He had power to show
The secrets of God's nature.   He Himself
Must lift the veil that hides Him from our view;
And coming forth reveal Himself to Man.
This is man's greatest need.   Amid the wrecks

That speak to us of his disordered powers,
This stands alone, as witness to the rank
In which he first was formed — a Creature, made
With the capacity of knowing God!
This mark is Man's alone. There is not one
Of all the creatures round him, that can share
This high distinction with him. As the eye
Is made for light, so Man is made for God.
He is his real end. In Him alone
His wants are met: his nature matched by One,
In whose unbounded fulness he can float;
And find his powers expanding as he moves.
Man has no need like this; no want so great,
As that which cries for God: and God no power
Like that by which He shows Himself to Man.
But how can this be done? Can Mortals look
On the Immortal One? Can Man sustain
The vision of God's glory? Can his eye
Endure the splendor of that cloudless light
In which Jehovah robes Himself? How then,
Can God be known? Can He reveal Himself
To creatures whom the vision would destroy?
Thus was all hope shut out: till God Himself
Came nigh to answer to His creatures' needs.
He would come forth, from the essential light,
In which He dwelt, as unincarnate God,
And show Himself to Man. He would put on
The garment of a nature, not His own;
That, through this tempered medium, men might
    look

And learn how God had yearned with tender love,
For His rebellious creatures ; how He could
To Man's estate stoop from His heavenly Throne,
Veil His Divinity in mortal flesh ;
And thus, in His humanity, become
The Kinsman of our race : and working out
The problem of the Evil on His Cross,
Make *that* the point where God and Man may be
At one again in Him ; bound with the tie
Of His great love which stooped to Death for this !

IX.

Thus, then, Creation took its fitting place,
Forerunner of Redemption.   Thus, among
Surrounding worlds the Earth came forth to be.
The chosen sphere, where the Redeeming God
Should take our form, and in it image forth
The Invisible to Man.   And does not this
Mark it, amidst its sisterhood of worlds,
With a peculiar glory ?   Is it not
The one distinction, that must ever shed
A halo round its history ?   For when
The Spirit brooded o'er the dark abyss,
And moulded into form the shapeless mass
That lay beneath, it was for this great end.
For this the Earth was finished ; and for this
The morning-stars sang out with shouts of joy.
For here, the Problem of the Good and Ill

Should find its true solution; and be laid
At rest forever. Here, the God of Grace
Should meet Man's sin, as sunbeams do the clouds,
And spread from this, through all surrounding
    worlds,
The more than rainbow glories of His love.*
For what God is, as now we see Him in
The work of Jesus Christ, He always was:
In His deep, tender, patient love the same.
Ready for His Self-Sacrifice; if thus
He could secure His creature's highest good,
By fixing their best love upon Himself.
And thus, the glory of His attributes,
Resides in Him, as rainbows in the light;
Unseen and unsuspected, till the cloud
Of Man's great sin encounters it. And then,
Justice and Mercy, Wisdom, Grace, and Truth,
Come forth in beauty, like prismatic rays,
And bend their arch of glory around the Cross.
And, through the course of everlasting years,
That glory shall continue, and diffuse
Its radiant light on all things. There we learn

---

* How clearly St. Paul states this. . . . . "God, who created all things by Jesus Christ, to the intent that now unto the principalities and powers, in the heavenlies, might be known by the Church, the manifold wisdom of God."—*Eph.* iii. 9, 10.

Now, when one thing is done *to the intent* that something else should follow, that other thing is the reason of its being done. Redemption, therefore, underlies Creation.

3

What God is in His nature.   There we see
How Love, in its unfolding, clears away
The darkness that remains, when every source
But this has been appealed to for its light.
Stronger than Power; it conquers where that fails.
Wiser than Wisdom; it resolves the doubts
Which Wisdom cannot reach, and sweetly blends
The varied colors in the light of Truth.

X.

But is there not in Nature, light enough
To show us what God is?   May we not read,
In lines of living light, His character,
As traced in all His works?   Do not the Heavens
Proclaim His glory?   Sun and Moon and Stars,
Are they not bright with radiance caught from
      Him?
Does not each dew-drop sparkle to His praise?
And is not tribute paid by all His works?
But Sin is in the world.   And countless wrongs
Repeat themselves each day; and Innocence
Goes to the wall and weeps.   And Vice and Crime
Flaunt it unblushingly before the Sun;
And the blasphemer, in his pride of place,
Reviles the name of God; and Want and Blood
Cry out unceasingly; but no reply
Comes from His presence.   And men vainly ask,
Is there a God who sees and hears all this?

And doubts, like armèd men, spring at the throat
Of trust in Him; and still, there is no voice
Nor any that gives answer. And we turn,
To scan the volume of His works, in vain.
We read no answer in the starry sky?
The hills are silent; and the Ocean's voice
Forgets its speech. For Nature has no skill,
To read this problem; and proclaim the truth,
That underlies these evils. It has lost
The thread to guide us through this labyrinth,
Into the open day; and tells us nought,
But of God's Power and Wisdom. And we ask
In vain, if He is Good? Does He regard
The creatures He has formed? Does He observe
The actions they perform; and bring the test
Of law, to try their nature? Does He put
A difference between them? or does Vice
Move Him the same as Virtue? Can He be,
Assailed by suffering, at the sight of that,
Which here, makes good men suffer? Does He
  hold
One uniform experience; or admit
The ebb and flow of feelings, such as swell
Within a Father's bosom, when he sees
A son's ingratitude? Alas! we know
Nothing of this, from what His works can teach!
He is, we know; and that we ought to make
His Will our Law. But then, what is His will?
Who shall instruct us here? Who show the way

Of access to His presence? May we come
With our own works; and thus expect to find
Acceptance with Him? Will He hear our prayers;
And in our darkness show us of His light?

XI.

"Athenians," — said the foremost man of Greece,
Foremost in wisdom, 'mong that mighty crowd
Of earnest seekers for the Good and True —
"Athenians! you must wait for One to come,
And teach you what to do. And He alone,
Who made you can do that." So, through the
     time
Of his great darkness, Man had felt for God,
Scarce knowing what he needed. Some great want,
Not apprehended, weighed upon his soul:
Which turned to seek for God, from the same cause
That plants do to the light. An inward need
Was on his spirit; and he blindly, turned
The tendrils of his powers, in eager search,
Around, beneath, above; if he might find
The One, fit Object, round which they might twine;
And twining round Him, lift himself again
Into the light. And who can say, how much,
Those earnest seekers of the Truth, obtained
By means we know not? Who can tell how far
The light of God shone in upon them? We
Know nothing of a thousand paths, by which,

God can gain access to the souls of men.
Did ever any seek His face in vain?
Did any turn to Him in ignorance
Of how He should be sought; and fail to find
That He was near to help? His Hand, unseen,
Has opened many a path, which, He alone,
Could point for man to tread; and turned the light
Of His own truth on many a darkened eye.
And thus we solve the problem, which the lives
Of Heathen sages offer to our thoughts;
Thus find the source, whence those of far-off times,
Plato and Socrates, and kindred souls,
Obtained the light, which glimmered on their path.
Perhaps they knew not whence its gleamings came?
Alas! how could they? Could you dream what
     source
The morn's gray dawning had if you were not
Familiar with the noon? And if *their* light
Was faint and cold and dim, it still revealed
Some glimpses of the Coming One, whose work
Is to give light to all men; and whose light,
Wherever found, leads only to Himself!
But, when all this is granted; it remains
That Sin has wrought a ruin so complete,
Throughout Man's nature, that the sense of want,
A void within, remains to testify,
He is not what he was. (A creature's wants
Define his character, and show his rank.
And, while created things fill up the need
  3 *

Of all the creatures round him, Man alone,
With all that they can give, looks out and asks
For something more than these. He feels the
 thrill
Of kindred with Divinity; and owns
Desires within, which, like a sense of wings,
Prompt him to rise; but, which, alas! afford
No power of flight. He cannot hope to scale
The height, from which he's fallen; or return
To his true sphere again. He has no power
To make the broken mirror of his soul,
Unite its shattered parts; and form again,
The image of His God which he has lost.
That work is God's. He, only, can repair
The ruins of the Fall. But how repair?
If worlds had been destroyed, He could renew.
If some destructive element had swept
Orders of beings into nothingness;
He could restore them with a word. But when,
The element of ruin is a Will
Self-poised, and acting from itself alone;
A will that chooses its own pathway, though
It leads to death; then, the restoring power
Must find its place within the souls of men.
It must assert itself, as — standing back
Of all the processes of thought — it yields
To the sweet force of some constraining love,
Which moulds its choice, and puts its impress on
Each power of thought and action. Therefore God,

To be this power, within the souls of men,
Came nigh in grace, and took on Him our form
Our nature took, that men might look and see
What He had always been : how thought and felt
About His creatures, when no eye could scan
The secrets of His nature.   How, in Him,
The tender, deep and self-forgetful love
Of Jesus, always dwelt.   How in His heart,
The thought of His Self-Sacrifice had place
Before all other thoughts.   And how with this,
Full in His view, He calmly, held His way
Through all that wondrous Life, up to the Cross ;
And there wrought out the problem of His love?
This, *this is God !*   Henceforth we see and know
His nature : He is Love.   His attributes
Are attributes of love.   The Cross of Christ
Unfolds it all ; and thus makes Him the power
Of that renewal, in the souls of men,
Which binds them fast, in loving loyalty,
Around His Throne, their Father and their God !

XII.

And thus we read the counsel that lay back
Of all Creation's works ; the Great Design
For which the Earth was made.   In lines of light,
We trace it in the volume of the Book ;
And own the purpose worthy of the God
Whose Thought it is.   Redemption is the pole,

Round which Creation is to crystallize
In joy and peace forever.　Here, we see
God's true unfolding of Himself.　The Cross,
Is yet, to be acknowledged as the first
And central figure of the Universe.
Here He shines truly forth.　Here He tells out
The secrets of His nature.　He is Love:
And Love is all embracing.　Everything
That marks His nature has its place in this,
And is a portion of it.　Neither Power,
Nor Truth, nor Justice, nor the attribute,
By which He hates all sin, expresses what
God truly is.　All these unite in Him;
But He is more than they: as is the Light
More than its spectral beams. They show, indeed,
Some glories of His nature.　But the Cross
Unites them all; and thus becomes the point
From which both Men and Angels shall survey
The truth about Him; and the wondrous tie,
That binds His creatures to Him.　To this Earth,
Redeemed and purged from all remains of sin,
Dwellers in other worlds shall flock to learn
The story of His Love: and here, survey
The scene of its great wonders.　Bethlehem,
And Nazareth; Calvary and the Mount
Of His Transfiguration; and the Well
Of Jacob, where He sat wearied, and taught;
The Garden, and the Tomb of Joseph, and
The Mount whence He ascended; and on which,

His feet shall rest again, when He returns,
To smite the Man of Sin, and take away
Out of His kingdom all things that offend ;
(These, and their kindred subjects, shall be made
Themes of discourse forever.   Here they'll say,
His infant form was in the Manger, laid.
He labored here, a lowly Carpenter :
Here He was tempted ; and a Crown of Thorns,
Was here set on His brow ; and here the Earth
Sustained His Cross ; and in this Tomb He lay,
When His great work was done; and here He rose,
Triumphant from the Grave, and broke the power
Of Death forevermore.   And thus through all
The periods of the Everlasting Age,
The Story of Redemption shall be found
The wonder of the Universe.   And Men
And dwellers in those far-off worlds of light,
Shall learn in this — the Switzerland of worlds —
The glory of the Lord : and think again
His own Great Thought, as it is mirrored forth
In His unfolding of Himself to Man !
The Earth, restored to its first purity,
And clothed once more with all the loveliness
That first adorned it, shall resume again
Its place in the vast sisterhood of worlds ;
And thus illustrate, throughout endless years,
The glory of the perfect work of Christ
That glory shall be on it, as a crown,
Forevermore ; and as the ages pass,

C

It shall be made — as God first meant it should —
The dwelling-place of men, who shall renew
Their generations on it; free from sin,
And in His love secured against its power.
The sunlight of His smile shall be its light;
And Want and Wretchedness shall be no more.
The curse shall disappear; and all the ills
That speak of its existence shall be known
As records of the Past: fossil remains
Of former periods, whose disturbing powers
Are laid at rest forever. Ignorance,
And Vice and Folly, Crime and Wretchedness,
Shall have a place no more. The widow's tears;
The orphan's cry; the friendless one's complaint;
The oppressor's wrong; shall all have passed away,
As troubled dreams before the waking hour;
And Righteousness and Peace, with their sweet
        smile,
Shall chase away the darkness of the Past.
And Earth shall yield her fruits without restraint;
And pour her full returns into the lap
Of men that own them, as a Father's gift,
And praise Him for His goodness. There shall be
No discord in the harmony that rolls
Its perfect song throughout Creation's works.
Through all the worlds, its rising notes shall swell;
Now high, now low; now ringing loud and clear,
To the grand key-note of Redeeming Love.
The Name of Jesus shall be everywhere,

The Name above all names ; and in its power,
All creatures shall be blessed forevermore.
The breeze shall speak it softly ; and the stars,
As they go forth, upon the silent march,
Of their unending course, shall proclaim
Its glory and its greatness.   Day to day,
Shall tell of its renown ; and as the Night
Puts on the splendor of its glittering crown,
It shall tell o'er the story of that Name,
And whisper of its sweetness.   Worlds on worlds
Shall add their voices ; and the countless ranks
Of beings that inhabit them, shall swell
The anthems of His praises, evermore.
O ! 't is not the full history of Earth,
That we record, through these six thousand years
Of sin upon its surface.   They are but
An eddy in its stream, that yet shall flow,
Broad'ning and deep'ning through unending years,
Of blessedness and joy; an episode
In the outworking of that wondrous Plan,
That is to bound its destiny. (And when
The cycle of Redemption is complete
It shall be found, that all the ills of sin,
Are but to be remembered, as a drop
Lost in the ocean of His boundless Love !

XIII.

Creation, thus, bears witness to some end,
Greater than it, that calls for it to be :

Some nobler reason, than material things
In all their splendor give.   And what could be
A reason so exalted, as the one
That underlies Creation ; and secures
God's Revelation of Himself to Man?
Sin shows us God, as clouds reveal the light.
And through its darkness, He moves on in grace ;
And from its ruin makes His grand display
Of the eternal purpose of His love.
And seeing what would be the dread result,
When Man had tried —(as try he surely would—
The experiment of Sin, selected this,
Least of the worlds, to be the Theatre,
Where it should work its dread conclusions out.
Here it should show its nature ; here display
Its full capacity of harm : and here,
He would, through Christ, bring glory out of shame ;
Life out of Death ; safety from ruin ; and
Unite all ranks of the whole family
In Heaven and Earth, in loving loyalty,
To the Almighty Throne ; and be Himself
The Source of all their blessedness ; the crown
Of Life and Glory, through the works of God !
All is in Christ ; centred in Him, alone,
The Manifesting God !   In Him the Light
Of this Great Thought was shrouded from the first ;
Hidden in Him alone ; and thence the rays,
Of its great glory streaming, bear His Name
To the remotest worlds.   All is in Him

As Light is in the Sun. (Behold the Scheme!
God's Revelation of Himself to Man,
And thus, to all His creatures; that in Him,
They may be saved from Sin's destructive power!
O! for the power to speak this wondrous Plan,
Where all may hear its wonders! Tell it out,
Ye dwellers in the nations! (Let the tongue,
Listless and dull, grow eloquent in this!
Speak of its greatness, as a Thought of God,
Before all other thoughts; and leading up
To all the glory that His works display!
Sing of it, O ye dwellers near the throne!
And in those far-off worlds, that circle round
Heaven's limitless expanse! Make it the theme
Of your rejoicing, as the ages pass:
And swell the chorus of a world, redeemed
By the same act that makes all creatures know,
And stand secure, in Jesus Christ the Lord!

4

CANTO SECOND.

THE UNFOLDING.

CANTO II.

ARGUMENT: Invocation. Earth at first the abode of other beings than Man. Reduced to Chaos. God's Spirit, brooding over the waters. Present order of things. Beauty of. Creation of Man. His distinguishing feature. Loneliness of. Creation of Eve. Adam and Eve in the Garden. Man in innocence. Innocence, not holiness. Difference between? True Freedom, what? Law, what? Man's accordance with Law. Must be tested. No character without a test. Seeming insignificance of real test. Adam's reasoning on. Choice. Result of. Good and Evil. Conscience. Sense of shame: fear: guilt. Hiding from God. Sentence on: Banishment from Eden. The First Promise. Effects of Sin on the animal Creation. Development of Sin. Cain and Abel. The Flood. Noah going out of the Ark. Rainbow. Covenant. Sin spreading. Babel. Dispersion of Man.

God did not leave Man thus. Designed to bring him back again. How? What God must be seen to be, before it can be done? Call of Abraham; greatness of results. One race set aside as witnesses for God. Israel in Egypt: David: Songs of: Progress in development of First Promise: Dispersion: Return: Man's Thoughts in History: God's: Testimony of Prophets to the Christ: Word Picture of: Angels' announcement of birth: Scene at Cradle: Mary, feeling of: Rejoicing. Wonder of Incarnation; Childhood of Jesus; agencies at work in; Spirit's teaching. Public ministry of Jesus: Character of: Meditations before the Cross.

40

THE UNFOLDING.

I.

O ! Thou Eternal One ! who art of Power
And Life and Light, the Uncreated Source;
From Whom are all things; in Whom all things
    stand;
And in Whose light, alone, we see the light;
Be near me while I write! My spirit fill
With Thine own Spirit. Let its radiance spread
Through all my powers, as through the dew-drop
    shines
The brightness of the Sun; that I may speak
Words, not unworthy of the Glorious Thought,
That moved within Thee, ere Creation was.

II.

Far back through ages, that we know not of,
Earth had its being, as the fit abode
Of other tribes, with different powers endowed,
From those that mark our race. But, from some
    cause,

— We know not of what nature — and by means,
As yet concealed from us, those tribes became
Outcasts from their inheritance; on which,
The hand of overthrow came sternly down;
And Earth, reduced to a chaotic state,*
Formless and void, lay waiting for the touch
Of the Life-giving Spirit, as it moved,
In brooding patience o'er the sluggish deep.
But, who may paint the Spirit's brooding work?
The silent going-forth of Power divine:
The gradual working of Omnipotence:
By which the strong foundations of the Earth,
Bearing the records of uncounted years,
Were wrought out from the ruins of the past!
How grand a thought it is! How much it tells,
That Restoration from a ruined state,
Is nobler than Creation! For a word
Accomplished that. God spake, and it was done.

Does this seem fanciful? Perhaps it is less so than it appears. In his admirable *Commentary on Genesis*, Dr. Murphy, Professor of Hebrew, Belfast, translates as follows:

"In the beginning, *God had created* the heavens and the earth.

"And the earth *had become* a waste and a void: (*Heb.,* *tohn vavohn :*) and darkness was upon the face of the deep."

Now, this seems to intimate, clearly enough, that it was not *created* "a waste and a void." It became so afterwards. So, too, we read in Is. xlv. 18 — "God Himself, that formed the earth and made it: He hath established it: He created it, not *in vain*" — i. e., *not tohn :* not a waste: not "without form."

But, when a ruined world awaits the touch
Of Restoration, He must work within
The Law of slow development, as broods
The Bird upon her nest. With patient care,
His Spirit brooded o'er the shapeless mass
That lay beneath the waters. Into them,
New principles must enter; and new laws
Be wrought within them; that new Life may come
And find a fitting home. And who can tell
The secrets of that brooding? Who can say
How long it was continued; or decide,
How much of all that makes the mystery
Of Earth's primeval strata, may be traced
As its direct results? We see, indeed,
That here is space and margin for the lapse
Of untold ages, in whose silent course,
The preparation for the coming birth
Of the new world, might be securely made.
But more we know not; more we need not know.
Then, when Earth's rock-ribbed storehouse thus
    was filled
With its uncounted treasures, for the use
Of coming generations, we behold
Creative power, in unconcealed display!
Then, from the womb of darkness, Earth was born.
Let Light be, said Jehovah, and Light was:
And by degrees, it took its garniture
Of grace and beauty, till it stood, disclosed
Perfect in loveliness: and God looked on

And called it very good — the fitting sphere,
For the great purpose, which He had in view!

III.

Call up the scene before you. See, what lines
Of perfect beauty, mark it! Every part
Is instinct with the presence of its God ;
And yields the worship of His own great thoughts,
In them incorporate. The Sun, by day,
Tells of His glory: and the Moon and Stars,
With gentler radiance, in His brightness shine,
All things are tuned to praise. The birds pour forth
Their joyous songs, which to His ear, assume
A meaning that we know not. Every flower
Presents the incense of its inner life,
Breathed out in perfumed worship ; and the trees
Bow down their heads, and all their branches wave
To the soft whispers of the evening breeze.
But Man, as yet appears not. See ! He lies
In glorious beauty on the new-formed Earth,
Just fashioned in the image of his God.
His form was perfect: but it had no life.
His beauty faultless ; but no living soul
Breathed into it expression. There he lay,
A fleshly statue, moulded to the Form,
Which the Redeeming God was to put on,
When He became incarnate. He was yet,
Only a statue ; when Jehovah came,

And breathed into his frame, the breath of lives;
And Man arose, possessing the same life
As other creatures round him ; and a Life
Kindred with God's, by which he has the power
To hold communion with Him ; to perceive
The glory of His thoughts ; to comprehend
His Nature ; and in harmony complete,
Respond to all His will : to see the truth,
Just as the eye sees light, as made for it,
And answering to its presence, everywhere.
This is Man's chief distinction.   Here he stands,
The Crowning Glory of the works of God.

I V.

And thus, Man stood, a power upon the Earth;
Thus absolute Dominion was the gift
Which God conferred upon him ; sovereignty
O'er all His works, below; authority,
As fully owned as it was gently urged.
The reins of government were in his hand ;
And all things owed obedience to his will.
But he was there alone.   Of all the tribes
That moved around him, there was found not one,
To offer him companionship, or be
A helpmeet for him.   None to take away
The sense of solitude, within his soul,
With the sweet ministry of love: or yield
Response to his desires, and enter in

To his communings with his secret self.
And answering to his needs, Jehovah said,
It is not good the Man should be alone,
I 'll make an helpmeet for him.   And at once,
A deep sleep fell upon him.   On the ground
He lay insensible ; yet seemed to see
The wondrous process, while the hand of God
Takes from his side, a rib, and closes up
With flesh instead thereof; and fashions it
Into a form of faultless beauty, like
Himself indeed, but more divinely fair.
And Adam, waking from his sleep, beheld
This wondrous vision, by the Hand divine,
Brought to his side ; henceforth to live and move
In his companionship, a second self;
His Bride, his heart's delight ; the only one
In all the universe, to make response
To thoughts and feelings, moving in his soul:
To share his joys; and, by the sharing, fill!
O! the deep rapture of his waking hour,
When Adam thus, received her ;(and beheld
An answering joy awakened in her soul!)
In what contrasted loveliness they move,
In converse sweet, through Eden's flowery groves!
Majestic beauty throned his ample brow;
And contemplation held her royal court,
With her attendant graces.   From his eye,
A living soul looked forth, that seemed to claim
Kindred with God, and in His right, to be

Exalted head o'er all His works on Earth.
Grace reigned in every motion, and controlled
The sense of power, beneath its gentler sway.
She seemed himself; though fashioned in a mould
Of fairer grace than he; and what appeared
Noblest and best in him, was tempered, with
A sweeter grace in her. The very air
That floated round her person, caught the glow
Of beauty from her presence; and became
Bright with her radiance. Was she not designed
His complemental self? For Man was formed,
A duplicate in being: and, each sex
Yields equal elements to make the sum
Of human nature, in the equipoise
Of its full powers. (Equal, not alike;
And not inferior, as some falsely teach.)
The gentler graces that attracted her
To all things sweet and lovely, were not less
Important in their sphere, than was the strong
And bolder outline of the character
God gave to him. Her beauty was the crown
Of his perfections; and his manly strength
The pillar of her beauty; each alike,
Finding completeness in the other's gifts.
And, as they moved through Eden, hand in hand,
In Love's sweet intercourse; or plucked the fruits
That hung, in sweet luxuriance on the boughs;
Or trained the vines, that waved their festooned
    sweets,

To greet them as they passed ; or breathed the soft
And balmy perfume of unnumbered flowers ;
All things told out their welcome. In the groves,
Birds warbled forth their greeting ; and with song,
And frolic motion testified their joy.
In low-toned cadences, the whispering breeze
Murmured a quiet joy; while from afar,
The sound of falling waters, lulled the ear
With strains of silvery music. The proud steed,
Neighed forth his welcome; while the fiercer tribes,
That Man's revolt has armed against himself,
Joined in the gambols of the playful kid.
The lion sported with the lamb; or walked
In stately motion by their side, as Eve
Laid a caressing hand upon his head.
All Nature spoke its gladness; and each tribe
Made contribution to the general joy. ⸠

V.

Thus, Man was made in perfect innocence.
In *innocence*, not holiness : for that
Grows out of spirit-beauty, which selects
Good for itself alone ; and rests therein,
Much as the magnet makes the needle rest.
It is the inflorescence of the soul ;
When, choosing Right and Duty for its own,
It opens in the sunlight of the Truth,
And blossoms into Liberty and Love.

But Man was made in innocence, and might
Have stood, as he was made; or carried up
The process of development, until
His choice was fixed, against all seeming good,
To be obedient to the Law of Truth;
And grow, in harmony with its demands,
Up to his highest excellence. He had
Full power to do so, if he chose. To act,
Against all motive, coming from without,
Or else, refrain from acting. He was free,
With that true freedom, whose distinction, is
Conformity to Law. And Law is naught,
But the unchanging principle of Right,
Which God finds in Himself. The harmony
Which its first utterance makes through all His
    works.
It is the Shadow of the Unseen God
Projected o'er His creatures; and they live
In peace and concord, as they live in it.
All things that are; the near and the remote;
Feel its controlling power. The very least
As not below it; and the greatest, as
Made great by it, alone. The violet
Thus holds communion with the far-off Sun;
And yields its beauty and its fragrance, back
As tribute to its power. So Man was meant,
To yield his answer to the Law, which sets
God in the centre of created things;
And builds up human character, in full

Accordance with His will.   He had the power,
Within himself, thus to decide for God,
As flowers might for the sunbeam, if there were
A reasoning soul within them, which could say,
I love the sunbeam.   It accords with all
The promptings of my nature.   Therefore, I
Open my bosom to its genial ray;
And breathe forth all my sweetness to its touch,
And live in it alone.   He might remain
In all the glory of his sinless state;
Choosing it as his own.   Or, he might break
The tie which bound him to his God; and go,
Careering downwards, in an unknown path,
To meet some unknown end.   He has the power.
And till he meets the question, and decides
Of his free choice for good; and fixes thus,
His state as under Law, his innocence
Is a negation only.   Beautiful;
But with no claim of moral worth; no tint
Of spirit-beauty, which selects the Good,
Because it loves it more than all things else.

VI.

Man therefore must be tested.   Will he keep
His loyalty to God; or step aside,
To a forbidden path, with no excuse,
But that it *was* forbidden?   There must be,
A test of character, that shall decide.

And graciously, this test was made to take
Such slight proportions, that it seemed to speak
A wantonness of spirit, in the act
Of disregarding it; while yet, it placed
The touchstone, to the metal of his will,
Disclosing what it was. "Of every tree,
Within the Garden thou may'st freely eat,
Excepting only one. Of this alone,
Thou shalt not take. It was not made for food;
And will not serve thy wants. Its fruit affords
Knowledge of Good and Evil; and if thou,
Presume to eat thereof, its penalty
Shall be enforced against thee. Thou shalt die."
So ran the First Command. And could a test
Less burdensome be given? Was it much,
That thus, one Tree should lift its fruitful boughs,
In test of Man's obedience? Was there not,
Eden's unbounded fulness, to supply
His every want? With all that could delight
The longing eye, or lusciously, repay
The most exacting taste; could Man make out
A case against his God, who thus, denied
One object to his touch? But here, began
Suggestion of the evil — made, no doubt,
In seeming innocence; but made no less,
By One who knew the evil: and could touch
Its secret springs of question and desire
That lead to outward action. What means this?
Why may it not be touched? Why should it spread

Its fruit before us if it speaks alone,
Of a forbidden act? Besides, the Tree
Is one to be desired to make one wise:
Speaks sweetly to the eye: and to the taste
Doubtless makes rich return. And if it brings
Knowledge of Good and Evil; is not that
Fruit fit for gods to feed on? And, are *we*
Alone to be denied it? Is it kind,
In the Creator, thus, to shut us out
From knowledge of this mystery? May we not
Eat of its fruit and live; although we know
The Good and Evil, too? Besides, it bears
No marks of aught so terrible. Does Death
Lurk in a thing so fair? But what *is* Death?
Some fearful evil, clearly: since it stands,
Fencing the Tree about, as penalty.
But *can* man die? Can this mysterious thing,
Gain access to a being, formed as we,
In God's own image? Does not God know all?
And if He dies not, may not we attain
To knowledge such as His; and feel the thrill
Of larger measures of Divinity?
But whether this or not; are we not free
To follow our own choice? To take what course,
May seem to us the best; without the fear
Of Law or Penalty to sway our choice?

VII.

Thus reasoned our First Parents; and at once,
The outward act betrayed the inward thought.
They took and ate! Eve first, as one beguiled
By subtle reasoning and delusive hopes
Of something loftier than her present lot,
Took the forbidden fruit; and in the glow
Of its first inspiration, sought to win
Her husband to her side. *She* was deceived!
But he, with knowledge of her act of sin,
Joined in the act—(choosing a creature's love,
Before the loyalty he owed his God.)
They took and ate. And lo! at once they found
The meaning of the penalty. They knew
The Evil and the Good; but found, alas!
The Good departed, while the Evil was
Their own, forevermore. The unseen tie,
Whose strong attraction bound them to their God,
And to all beautiful and lovely things,
At once was severed. Deep within, they feel
The spirit-wound: for Faith in God was gone;
And Love gave place to Fear; and filial trust
Yielded to sudden dread. The blush of shame
Burned on their cheeks, when they looked on and
    saw
Their robe of innocency, torn away;
And all the glory of their first estate
Laid in the dust forever. There was now

5*

A strange, unwonted sense of coming ill;
A deep unrest; a fluttering sense of fear;
And Paradise was Paradise, no more.
Its glorious beauties all remained the same;
The trees were still as grand; the flowers as sweet;
The birds as beautiful : the air as full
Of melody and fragrance as before.
But they perceived it not. The sense of guilt
Was in their heart; coming to them, in dreams;
And peopling e'en the silence of the night;
With forms of evil, never known till then.
It started into shape before their eyes;
Made dumb things speak; and, in the thought of
        God,
Shook them with strange commotion, clothing Him,
With all the human elements of wrath,
For their transgression. And they slunk away
To seek a shelter 'mid the friendly trees.
All things accused them. Nature felt the stroke
Of Man's rebellion; and in all her powers,
Arrayed herself to visit the deep wrong
Of Sin upon his head. Its sudden jar,
Made discord in her music — bringing forth
Harsh notes of sorrow, suffering and pain,
Where God intended peace. And still, she tells'
The story of his guilt, which finds a voice
In all her creatures. Are they not involved
In his transgression ? Do not its results
Subject them to a servitude, whose chains

They never, else had borne? Are they not made,
Subject to vanity? And as they turn
To Man, their master, with imploring eyes,
It is as if they charged him with the wrongs,
They suffer at his hands! And who can feel
That he is guiltless here? Or, feeling this,
Restrain his exultation at the thought
Of the mute prophecy, in which she waits
The Coming Day, which shall at last, restore
Her lost inheritance — lost not by her —
And, with the glorious liberty, decreed
The sons of God, shall once more, make her free?

VIII.

The brightness of the day had lost itself,
In the delicious coolness of the eve;
When God came down to judgment. Yesterday,
They would have hailed His coming. Now, alas!
They stand, abashed before Him; for the sense
Of guilt within the soul, interprets God,
According to its nature; and they seek
A shelter from His presence, though He comes
To give them hope in ruin; and to twine
The words of promise round their fallen state!
Adam! where art thou? said the Voice Divine.
I was afraid, he answered, when I saw
That I was naked; and I hid myself.
Who told thee, thou wast naked? Hast thou done,

What I commanded thee, thou should'st not do ?
Did I not tell thee, Death was in that fruit?
And now its doom is on thee, evermore !
For dying, thou shalt die.   The earth shall yield,
Unwillingly, its produce to thy toil.
And thorns and thistles shall proclaim the curse
Thy sin has brought upon it.   All thy days,
Thou shalt in sorrow eat thereof, till thou
Return to dust again.   For out of it,
Thou at the first wast taken.   Dust thou art,
And unto dust shalt thou return !   But still,
Not unrelieved thy sentence shall be found ;
The Woman's Seed shall bruise the Serpent's head.
And out of this great evil shall be brought
Redemption from all evil.   But for thee,   ·
Eden is home no more.   Thou must go forth
To till the ground, and subjugate the earth,
Deprived of her first fruitfulness by thee !
And from its beauteous borders they went forth,
With slow, reluctant, and despairing steps.
For, should they see their Eden-Home, no more ?
No more, for them, its glorious flowers should
      bloom,
Or balmy air delight ! Its luscious fruits,
Whose rich profusion tempted every sense,   .
Should yield their stores no more ; but rugged toil
Win its unwilling produce from the Earth.
And as they linger near its sacred bounds,
Behold ! the Cherubim commenced their watch ·

About its borders ; and the flaming sword
Kept fiery guard around the Tree of Life !
Yet, not unmixed with mercy was the stroke
Of judgment which o'ertook them.   For the fruit
Of Life's fair Tree had power to give them life.
Life, in the flesh : Life, while revolving years
Added their burden to the weary frame
Longing for rest, but sharing evermore,
An immortality of dying life !
Thus they went forth from Eden ; knowing not
The future that awaited them ; alone,
And unprotected, save as girt about,
With the invisible, but strong defence,
With which their higher nature hedged them round.
And much they needed it : for Nature's tribes
Ceased from their gentle ministry to Man,
When he forgot allegiance to his God !
That was the tie that bound them.   His revolt
Snapped it asunder ; and to active life,
Summoned ferocious passions, which had else,
Slumbered in quietude.   The Lion leaped
Upon the harmless kid, that but of late,
Had gambolled with him, on the flowery mead.
The timid dove fled, trembling, from the hawk,
That fiercely struck it down. The lamb, that cropped
The flowery herbage, trembled with a sense
Of fear, unknown before, as stealthily,
The tiger crouched to leap upon his prey.
All things attested the new element

Of Evil in the world : and showed that Sin,
Breaking the tie that bound Man to his God,
Destroyed the harmony of all His works !

I X.

And thus they stood outside of Paradise,
There to return no more.   They could not know
What glorious germs of truth were folded up,
In the First Promise : as some lovely flower
Is folded in its seed.   They knew, indeed,
That God had interposed.   But in what form,
That interference would reveal itself :
What was the meaning of the Woman's Seed ;
The bruising of the Serpent's head ; or how
Their Maker would accomplish this ; was yet
Involved in darkness.   They must learn to wait.
And thus time passed ; and as the race increased,
Sin varied its disclosures, till the Earth
Opened its mouth, and drank in Abel's blood,
Shed by his brother's hand.   And Time passed on,
And wickedness increased ; and men became
Corrupt upon the Earth ; and in the course
Of their three times three hundred years, attained
Gigantic stature in their wickedness.
Then judgment came upon them ; and the Flood
Swept them away ; and o'er its troubled waves,
The Ark rode peacefully, and bore within,
The seed of a new race, which should possess

The Earth again, when from its watery grave,
It should arise, to run once more, the course
Of God's forbearance with the sin of Man !
Slowly and reverently, at God's command,
Noah went forth, to repossess the Earth.
Silence was all around ; for of the vast
And teeming multitudes, that lately thronged
Its busy surface, he alone remained !
He and his family : and in the hush
Of its deep solitude, he offers up
His tribute of adoring love and praise.
And as the patriarch bows himself in prayer,
Jehovah answers, — There shall be, no more,
A flood of waters to destroy the earth.
Behold ! I set my Bow within the clouds ;
And it shall be, through everlasting years
A sign of this my covenant with the earth,
And every creature on it.   When I bring
A cloud upon the earth, the bow shall be
Within the cloud; and, bending its bright arch
Of glory o'er its darkness, sweetly speak,
In smiles and tears, of peace from God to Man !
And, as He spoke, lo ! bursting from the clouds,
A glorious vision bent its radiant arch
Of many-colored light, above the spot
Where Noah stood and worshipped; trembling
        there,
As if in ecstasy, at the delight
Its presence would procure the sons of men.

So, through the ages, it has been for God,
A witness unto Man.   Children at play,
Start up with joyous shout, and clap their hands,
In welcome of its coming.   On his couch,
The sick man turns, to gaze with longing eye,
Upon its loveliness; and think, perhaps,
Of that bright Home beyond its glowing belt
Where sickness never comes !   The old man leans
Upon his staff to gaze; and reverently,
Reads God's own writing in a thing so fair.
All Nature seems at peace.   The birds pour out
Their sweetest songs; as if they felt the joy
Its presence sheds around; while purer light
Seems to invest each object where it shines !
And thus, the Earth was saved, for endless years;
And God's own token of the Covenant,
Set in the heavens to tell how sure it is !

X.

Not long remembered, was the lesson taught
By this sharp stroke of judgment.   Sin went on
In its development; and spread its blight
And desolation round it.   Men presumed
To form conspiracies upon the earth,
Against the God of Heaven.   Defiantly,
They sought to make a name, and rear a Throne,
Whose universal power should send its sway
Throughout the ages; and embrace in one,

The nations of the earth.   And so, they laid
Its strong foundations ; and presumed to rear
Its massive walls, when God came near to check
The impious design, and scattered them,
Abroad upon the earth.   And, from that hour,
Babel has stood, to all succeeding time,
A monument of folly, and of guilt ;
A synonymn for every thought of Man
That seeks to be a God unto itself.

XI.

But did God leave him thus ?   Did He consent,
That Man should carry out his own designs,
Without the counter-working of the Thought
Which, in the end, should bring the wanderer back,
To His own arms again ?   No.   From the first,
The Counsel of Redemption was at work
To compass this design ; as through the night,
He silently prepares the coming day.
For, if Man's spirit is to be redeemed
From Sin's control ; not in Creative power,
Is the redemption found.   By moral force
Alone, is spirit moved ; and that is gained
By slow degrees, as moral qualities
Display their presence.   Would you lay again
The strong foundation of a child-like trust,
Once overturned?   Such trust is born of love.
And Love springs out of qualities that win

6

The spirit's homage. And, ere we can stretch
The arms of our affection out to God,
And rest upon His bosom ; He must be
The Father of our spirits ; known as such,
For us His rebel children. He must show
How He had borne the burden of our guilt,
Upon His heart, when we had lost the power
To comprehend our guilt. He must abide
In patient waiting, for the end in view ;
And lay the long procession of events,
That are to bring it in. From first to last,
The work is His alone. And when He stands
In the full light of His accomplished Thought ;
When His great love has wrought out its design ;
Until it puts its crown of glory on,
In Jesus Christ the Manifested God ;
Then shall that love be found to be the power
Of new-creation in the souls of men ;
Awaking there, the thrill of a new life,
That sweetly answers back God's Fatherhood,
With the new sense of Sonship ; and that loves,
Because His love constrains it. Therefore, He,
Not in His works, but in His character
Must show Himself to Man. He must remove
The misconceptions Sin had introduced
About Himself; and show how, from the first,
He calmly waited for the day to come
When Man should know, and knowing trust His
    God.

Meanwhile, He poured His royal bounties out,
In Nature's countless ministries for good ;
Content to be belied, e'en in His gifts ;
Bearing the Calvary of His patient love ;
Rejoicing still, that, e'en at such a cost,
He could become Redemption to the souls
That Sin had severed from their trust in God.
This was His meaning ; and the ages were
The stepping-stones, on which Jehovah moved,
In tracing out His Great Design for Man.

XII.

Its lines advance ; but only as the dawn.
Grows to the perfect day. No sudden change
Marks its development : as through the gloom,
There steals a trace of light, so faint and dim,
You almost question if it *is* the light ?
And yet it glows and deepens and extends,
Until it floods the landscape with its beams.
Thus unobserved, among the sons of men,
Was God's great movement, in the going forth
Of an old man, from Home and Fatherland,
To dwell—he knew not where. No sudden change
Told of the deed ; and yet, the morning dawn
Was speeding onward, from the hour when God
Called Abram from his home and Father's house.
He had no sign, but God's express command ;
No token but his faith : and yet he went ;

Went without question ; leaving all to Him
Who bade him go. " Look now and count the stars,
If thou canst number them ; " and he looked up ;
And as their glittering host marched silently,
Across the sky, the Voice Divine replied,
" *So shall thy seed be.*"   And the patriarch's heart
Breathed, odor-like, its sweet *amen* to God ! *
In him and in his seed, the nations were
To be completely blessed.   The Woman's Seed,
In Whom all promises would be fulfilled,
Should come through him; and all the nations were
To own him for a blessing.   What, if yet,
He had no child ?   Was not the Promiser
Equal to what He promised ?   Would He not
Make good His word ; and vindicate the faith,
That rested on it ?   He would calmly wait,
And go forth in the path He bade him tread.
And, as he went, the light before him grew ;
The scene extended ; and his vision ranged
O'er wider fields of truth, until he stood
In the full glory of that perfect trust
That gives its best to God.   And all the light
That floods the world to-day; each hope that glows
With immortality, shines on our path,
As the unfolding of that first, faint beam

---

* It is a beautiful thing, I think, that the Hebrew renders
this, " he *amened* Jehovah "—*i. e.* was *fixed and stable and
sure* in his mind, toward Him.   And this is believing.

That, scarcely, tinged the sky, when he went forth
To seek a heavenly country. It was all
Embraced potentially, in that command;
Much as the acorn shuts, within its folds,
The oak of centuries. From him, has sprung
A line of witnesses for God, by whom
His truth has been preserved; and every age
Has seen that line sweep onward, telling o'er
The story of God's dealings in the past,
And looking for the future; when the scroll
Of all the promises shall be unrolled,
And Israel stand, redeemed, regenerate,
The royal nation, 'mid Earth's ransomed tribes,
Filling the world with fruit. And thus, one race
Was set apart as chosen witnesses
For God and for His Truth, evermore!

XIII.

A thousand years sweep onward; and the seed,
Promised to Abraham, had now become
A mighty nation; ruling in the midst
Of the surrounding nations, with a sway
That all respected; tempered, wise and strong.
A strangely chequered history was theirs!
Captives in Egypt, they had groaned beneath
The rod of their Oppressors; but their God,
Their Fathers' God, came forth in their behalf;
And broke the power that bowed them to the dust;

And brought them out, and with a mighty hand,
Gave them a heritage within the Land,
Promised their Fathers; and from all their tribes,
Selected one, to take the kingly place,
Ere royalty was dreamed of. From its midst,
One Family was taken; and from that,
One Man selected, as the Special Head.
Of all the tribes, thro' whom the Woman's Seed,
Was to come forth. And David sits, enthroned,
The Chosen Head, collecting in Himself,
The scattered rays of promises that told
Of the Deliverer from the Chains of Sin;
Celestial visions on his spirit rose;
And heavenly harmonies, to him unknown,
Moved rapturously, within; and tides of thought,
Whose living power he knew not, heaved and fell,
As waves do in the Ocean, sending out
Their eddies to the farthest bounds of Life.
He touched his harp; and through the nations rolled
A tide of song, rich, glorious and divine.
It sparkled with the light of every hope,
That glows within the heart. It took the shade
Of every thought of sadness; and it touched
The electric cord, that binds the soul of man,
To Life, beyond the Grave; and waked the thrill
Of an immortal hope. In every stage,
Of human life, his melodies Divine,
Have been the stay of thousands. They have come,
Like angel-forms, to strengthen us when weak;

To comfort us when sad; and lift the veil,
That Sin has dropped, betwixt the soul and God.
And thus the lines of Progress were defined;
And God's First Promise shaped the instruments
Of its fulfilment, in the Woman's Seed:
The Root and Offspring of the royal head
Of Judah's honored line : The Central Point,
Of all the glory of the works of God!

XIV.

Time rolled away; and on its tide was borne
What seemed the wreck of all that went before.
For Israel was dismembered; and its tribes
Were carried captives, into other lands,
Whence they returned, no more. The nation's sin
Cast off the crown of glory from their head;
Broke down the wall of their defence; and left
The nation helpless, in the midst of foes.
Judah remained. For yet, a little while,
It kept its loyalty to God; and held
Its place among the nations. But the taint
Of their idolatry diffused itself
Among the chosen people. All the past,
Seemed a forgotten history. No more
The nation's heart beat truly for its God;
But joined in idol-worship; and to things,
Which their own hands had fashioned, gave the
        praise,

Which should have been the perfume of their hearts,
To Him who gave them all.   Then came the stroke
Of Judgment on them; and by Babel's streams,
They hung their harps upon the willows, and
In bitterness of spirit, mourned the sin,
That drove them from their home.   The evening
          breeze,
Sighing in mournful cadences, awoke
Responsive murmurs from the strings, which once
Made joyous music unto Israel's God.
And memories of their home and native-land,
Moved tenderly, within them; while the tear
Stealing, unconsciously adown the cheek,
Told of the heart's deep secret; as the drops
That Night suspends on grass and leaf and flower,
Tell of the absence of the Sun, whose heat
Creates this crystal jewelry.   And thus,
Seasons revolve; and to the years assigned
For their captivity, the end drew near.
And men return, as hoary-headed sires;
Feeble and bent with age, who in the flush
Of early childhood, joined the captive train,
Not knowing what it meant.   Yet from the land
Of their dispersion, Judah must come back
That in the line of David might be born
David's anointed Head; the Woman's Seed
Fulfiller of the promises; for Whom, .
All things that are, exist.   And thus, behind
The rise and fall of nations; and the powers

That men assign as leading up to these;
Is found a Something, greater than them all.
Working unseen; spreading itself, unknown;
Pervading motives; leading on to acts;
And shaping human history.. And when,
Men seem the freest from all outward strain;
Self-poised and self-determined; they are but
The chisel that rough-hews the grand designs
Of a controlling God, whose purposes
Run through the changes, which, like ocean-waves,
Sweep o'er the face of nations. Kings and Lords,
Captains and Counsellors, believe themselves
The architects of History: building here;
Destroying there; and thinking that *their* plans,
Were the great ends involved. Will they not learn
That History has a meaning? That it marks
The mile-stones, in the progress of the Race,
Towards God and Freedom? That the helpers here,
However lowly, work in line with God,
Although they know it not? And if their thoughts
Reach not beyond the acts in which they moved;
The acts alone are theirs; while the results
Work for the furtherance of the General Scheme,
By which the Evil shall be met at last,
And put away forever, by the might
Of God's transforming love, as seen and felt
In Christ, the Coming One. And so, I look,
With awe and gratitude, on the return
Of Judah's thousands to their native land.

The Promise calls them back! The Woman's Seed
Unborn, awaits the progress of events,
Which, in the fulness of the time, should be
The sign of His appearing.   And they come,
Not knowing *why* they come.   A Heathen king
Prepares their way before them; knowing not
The secret spring, from which his action flows.
And Judah seeks his native home, once more,
That in the Land of Promise might be born,
The World's Restorer, as the prophets said.

X V.

Meanwhile, through ages past, prophets and seers
Had told of His appearing.   They had gone
Like painters to the canvas, sketching there,
Some feature of His character and work.
And still, as ages passed, they came and stood
By the prophetic page; and silently,
And, without comprehension of the truth,
Their words embodied, carried out some line
Of the Great Portrait, which unconsciously,
Was growing into form beneath their touch.
And now, it stands complete!   Lo! here it is!
The Marvel of all marvels! God's Great Thought,
Before the worlds were made; now spoken out,
On the prophetic page, and taking form
In the Restorer of the World from Sin.
See! what a heavenly light beams round Him, here!

Light, self-derived! Light, streaming from Himself!
The page grows luminous that tells of Him.
From Him comes forth the glory; and in Him,
Resides the secret power that lifts His name,
Above all other names; and round His brow,
Wreathes that celestial halo, which suggests
How radiant are men's thoughts concerning Him!
Thus, for four thousand years, His portrait grew
To its divine completion. Line by line,
Was added to its outline: till the page
Of Inspiration glowed with this one thought.
The glory of the Coming One! And there,
It stands, to-day, the *Wonder of the World!*
His Name; His Lineage; Office; place of birth;
His character — in all the radiant lines
That centre in Him, from opposing sides,
Godhead and Manhood — all were here portrayed
In lines of living light. His death for Sin;
His rising from the grave; and the results
That should flow on through everlasting years,
From His great work, are all distinctly lined
In this Word-Portrait, which the Book of God
Holds up before our view; that, when He came,
The watchers for His coming, might exclaim,
Lo! This is He! The Woman's Promised Seed!
The World's Restorer! He has come at last!

XVI.

And now the Time has come; and angels tell
To shepherds, watching on Judea's plains,
The story of His birth. Was it not meet,
That Heaven should send forth its angelic throngs,
To greet His coming, in this lowly guise,
Whom they had worshipped as the Lord of all?
And now draw near; and with a gentle tread,
Approach His Manger-Cradle! See! what grace
Is throned upon His brow! What loveliness,
Marks every feature! How the living soul
Looks through the clear depths of His radiant eye,
Unconscious of the mystery of His birth!
And yet it speaks of something, which, till now,
Was never joined to one of woman born!
See there, the Virgin-Mother! What a light
Gleams in her eye! What reverence blends with
    love,   ●
As, looking down upon that Infant-Form,
Nestling upon her bosom, she recalls
The secret of His birth! Does she not know
The mystery that attends it? Was He not,
Fashioned within her? Nourished from her frame?
Was not His form, the miniature of her's?
Beneath her bosom, was it not sustained?
And yet, whence came its germ? O! was it less
Than a direct exertion of His power,
Who formed the First Man from the dust? If now,

He builds the Second, in the Virgin's womb,
Is not the power as truly His ? The act
As much divine ? Is He not moving on,
To rear the Temple, where The Christ shall dwell,
In manifesting God ? And *she* has part
In this great wonder! *She* is chosen, out
Of all earth's countless thousands, as the one,
In whom the Lord of Glory shall put on
His garniture of flesh! And as this thought
Rises within her, with a hush of awe,
She looks upon her Babe : and bows her head,
In lowly worship to the Lord of all!
How reverently, the Wise men from the East,
Led by that wondrous Star, display their gifts ;
Prophetic of His Character and Work !
And now the Shepherds enter! It is true,
Just as the angels said. The promised sign
Is here, before them. In the Manger, lies
The new-born Saviour : and with joy, they tell
The tale, the angels told ; and to their flocks,
Return again, with wonder in their hearts,
And songs upon their lips. The Christ has come !
Sing ! O, ye ransomed nations ! Tell it out,
Ye dwellers in the islands ! Let the Sea
Lift up its voice ; and Earth, through all her
  coasts,
Ring out the joyous notes, *The Christ has come !*
The Christ! Ordained before the World was made !
The Christ ! Enwrapping all the purposes

7

Of God, within Himself: alike if they
Reach back to the past ages, or spread out
Through the unending future.   All, in Him,
Attain their full unfolding, for He is,
All these, within Himself.   The First: The Last:
The Soul; The Seal of all the promises;
Beginning of Creation, and its Crown.
The vital Breath of all God's works; Himself,
Including all things!   *He has come at last!*

XVII.

Here let me pause and wonder!   In this Birth,
I see the blossom of the Germ of Hope,
Which God, first, planted in the Soul of Man!
The bud unfolding, is the Living Christ!
Here, He comes near to help me!   Here He takes
My nature into union with Himself.
Here He becomes my Brother!   Taking part
In all my weakness, yet without my sin.
But here, my sin is pressing on His heart,
As bringing Him to this.   Why lies He here?
What overpowering need led up to this?
What but His creatures' ruin?   On His heart
He took the burden of my sin.   My guilt
Went to His soul, and wrought Him grief and pain;
Which lay upon Him, as a Father's grief
For his rebellious child!   And so, He came,
Out of the glory of His own estate;

And put the vestments of our nature on ;
And, as the Babe of Bethlehem, lay down
In this, His Manger-Cradle ; passing through
Each stage of our humanity, that there,
He might reveal God's wondrous love to Man.
He told it out through life ; and, on the Cross,
Completed its revealing.   Here we learn
The fulness of its meaning.   He could give
Himself, a Sacrifice ; and thus, become
The power of a new-life, in guilty souls.
And from the first, this was the scene which rose
Before His vision.   Ere the worlds were made,
Redemption was His purpose.   He foresaw
The entrance of man's sin : and all the ills
That follow in its train.   The grand results,
Which, rainbow-like, should bend their glowing
      arch,
Above our fallen race, when the dark cloud
Of Man's transgressions, had become the means
Of showing forth the riches of His Love,
Were all before His view.   The angel's Song
Was His fixed purpose everlastingly.
He saw the Babe of Bethlehem ; and traced
The pathway, which the Man of Sorrows trod :·
And as He looked, He owned the thrill of joy,
Which full Redemption gives ; although He knew,
The Manger and the Cross alike were His.

XVIII.

O! for the power to lift the veil, which hides
The secret of His Childhood! How we yearn,
To trace some mark of His expanding soul,
And learn the processes, through which He gained
The knowledge of Himself. Was it the smile,
Born of a Mother's love, that first awoke
His consciousness of love? Was it the truths,
Taught at her knee, that started, in His thoughts
Those undefined conceptions of Himself,
That hovered near the mystery of His Birth,
Without the power to read it? Who can tell
The heavenly agencies that moved within,
And thrilled Him with a living sympathy,
With all the works of God? There was a voice,
Deep; solemn; musical; in Nature's moods,
That told Him of her mysteries. Sunset clouds
Glowed with the glory of a God, unseen,
But shadowed in His works. The evening breeze
Whispered His Name, in cadence soft and low;
The lilies of the field spoke of His care;
While every bird, that warbled forth its song,
Became a witness for Him. Day by day,
Made new disclosures to Him; and the Night,
As she put on her coronet of stars,
Told of the many mansions, where should dwell
The bands of His Redeemed. The ripening grain
Spoke of the Coming Harvest; and the tares,

That grew in the same field, in silent tones,
Told of the Separation, yet to come.
And thus, the volume of His Father's Works
Revealed its hidden meaning: while His Word
Brought tribute to His Mission. Here He learned
God's thoughts about Himself; the Great Design,
He came to carry forward ; and the ends,
He should accomplish.   Hence, the Spirit took
The doctrines He should teach, which blossomed
 out,
From the dry stem of the Prophetic Word,
When *He* became their meaning. Morn by morn,
His Heavenly Teacher wakened Him to hear.*
Truth rose upon Him, as the morning light
Dawns on the landscape.   And with its increase
He yielded up Himself, to each demand,
It made upon Him ; till its subtle power
Pervaded His whole Being, and each thought

* Very striking is the testimony borne by the Prophets to this great truth. " *The Lord God hath given Me the tongue of the learned; that I might know how to speak a word in season to him that is weary. He wakeneth morning by morning: He wakeneth mine ear to hear as the learned. The Lord God hath opened mine ear, and I was not rebellious,* neither turned away back.

"I gave My back to the smiter; and My cheek to them that plucked off the hair. I hid not My face, from shame and spitting." — *Is.* l. 4-7.

It was all made known to Him by the Holy Spirit ; who " *morning by morning,*" wakened Him to hear !
 7 *

Grew in the light.   Celestial harmonies,
Unheard by all beside, attuned His soul,
In sweet accord with all the will of God.
The secrets of the past eternity
Were all revealed before Him; and He saw,
In the clear sunlight of the Thoughts of God,
The work He came to do, just as it stood
Before His vision, ere He stooped to take
The garb of our humanity.   And as
The great conception rose before His view
He sweetly breathed His spirit's one response —
I come to do what in Thy Book I trace :
Lo! I delight to do Thy will, My God!

XIX.

And now He stands prepared.   But who can trace
The lines of beauty and of glory, which
Attend Him in His work?   He spoke; and men
Listened with wonder; for His words came forth,
Fresh as the sunbeam, shedding heavenly light,
On every theme He touched.   He never stood
Below His subject, working up His way,
From premise to conclusion; but as One
Who was Himself the Truth, He told it out,
In words divinely clear.   There was an air,
Of majesty about Him, which bespoke
Authority to teach; yet clothed itself,
In such transparent truthfulness, that men

Allowed His claim, e'en when it soared the most.
He drew not from the Schools; and nothing owed
To those that went before; but stood alone,
As truly as the sunbeam, when it comes
Into the midst of darkness; shedding light,
As from its Central Source. He spoke of God;
His Fatherhood;· His love; His tender care
For all His creatures; and His words have, since,
Been sounding through the ages, telling o'er
The story of that love. The humblest flower,
Lifting its bright eye on us, from the sod,
In tremulous emotion, seems to speak
Of Him who clothed it, in a dress so fair.
The birds repeat the story; and sing out,
With gushing sweetness, of His constant care.
An atmosphere of love surrounds the world;
And though they know it not, His creatures move
And have their being in it. All His works
Acquire new meaning in the glorious light
Which Jesus shed around them. Nothing, now,
Wears the same aspect, as before we knew
The story of the Fatherhood of God;
And how, in the humanity of Christ,
All men are brethren. In His wondrous life,
There was a beauty, answering to His word.
Pure, holy, harmless, separate from sin;
He felt the thrill of tenderest sympathy
For those whom Sin had ruined. See Him stand,
In the calm majesty of silent power,

As round about Him, lay the halt, the blind,
The lunatic, the palsied, the possessed;
No word was spoken; yet He felt the plea
Of silent eloquence, with which their need
Spoke to His heart. For were they not His work?
His creatures, ruined, but His creatures still?
Did He not bear their sickness on His heart?
Was not their grief His sorrow? Did He not
Feel, as His own, the burdens they endured?
And so He answered to their wordless plaint,
And healed them all. At His enabling word,
The blind received their sight; the flush of health
Glowed in the leper's cheek; the dumb man spake;
The dead were raised; and devils fled away,
From those whom they possessed. He wiped the
　　　tears
From weeping eyes, and answered to the touch
Of every human sorrow. In the midst
Of men, oppressed with want and carking care;
Weary and heavy-laden; knowing not
The secrets of their burden; He stood up,
And spoke the secret of His Gospel out,
Come unto Me, and I will give you rest!
Death reigned on every hand; but *He* was Life;
And came to give that life. He was Himself,
The Resurrection; and in Him alone,
Death loses all its power. And so He came,
Revealing God, while He seemed only Man;
And lifting Man up to the Thought of God!

There was a faultless harmony in all
He did, and said and was.   No discord marred
The music of His life, which flowed along
In its divine perfection ; and men looked
And saw a perfect character, displayed
In all the actions of His wondrous Life!
He was the Central Figure, in the light
Of the Prophetic Word ; the Pearl of price ;
Giving its best and hidden beauties out,
When held at different angles to the Sun !
And thus He lived ; unfolding day by day,
More of the truth ; moved by a perfect love ;
And yielding its full answer on the Cross !

X X.

Here I would stand and gaze ; for here I learn
The secrets of His nature.   Here I find
The glory of His being.   Man can mount
Up to the thought of Power ; and thrill beneath.
Its inspiration.   He can comprehend
Wisdom and Justice, Holiness and Truth.
The tenderness of Pity, He can feel ;
And move responsive to the touch of Wrath.
And these belong to God.   They enter in,
As factors of His Being.   They are parts
Of the grand total of His character ;
Modes of His Spirit's action ; touching not
The secret of His nature.   But the Cross

F

Reveals *Himself.* It shows me how He is,
At once the Wisdom and the Power of God,
In His Self-Sacrifice. It lifts the veil,
That hides the inner workings of a Love,
Deep, tender, self-forgetful; thinking not
Of its own pleasure; living for the sake
Of those whom it can bless; becoming thus,
The power of a new life, in guilty souls;
Dispensing good, as His one answer to
Each form of ill around Him; breathing out
Blessings for curses, as the Sandal-Tree
Perfumes the axe that wounds it.* O! the Cross
Illustrates all; and blends them all in one,
Broad stream of light; and darkness flees away;
And every problem finds its solvent here;
And Sin is met; and judged and put away;
That it may spread no more. And every doubt
Looking thereon, forgets its power to harm,
And sits transformed before the Cross of Christ!
Here let me stand and gaze; for here my soul
Is melted and subdued. The things of earth

* I do not know whether this is my own thought or not.
Sir William Jones has preserved an exquisite verse of Persian
poetry, which is as sweet as the odor of this tree. It is this:

> The Sandal-Tree perfumes when riven
> The axe that lays it low:
> *Let man that hopes to be forgiven,*
> *Forgive and bless his foe.*

Is there not room enough for both comparisons?

Here seem to fade away, and leave behind
The deathless issues of Redeeming Love !
That Cross is not, as men believed it once,
The place of Shame and Death ; but all aglow,
With the indwelling and outshining light
Of majesty and splendor.   For it is
The meeting-place of Justice, Mercy, Truth.
Here they link hands together ; here combine
To write the glorious sentence, *God is Love*,
And wreathe it as a crown upon His brow.
Here God comes nigh to tell me what He is.
Here He reveals Himself: here stoops to take
His rebel-child into His arms again.
Rebel no more ; but conquered by the might
Of His omnipotent, ungrudging, love.
This, this is all I need ; only to know
The Cross of Christ, in its transforming power.
Long had the thought of God come to my soul
Through a false medium ; and He seemed to me,
Hard, cold, unfeeling ; watching o'er my way,
To find account against me.   For my sin
Had dug a gulf, I had no power to cross :
And thrust me from His presence ; clothing Him
With all the enmity that had its seat,
In my own heart, alone.   My faith was gone ;
I could no longer, trust.   For my great sin
·Came and sat down betwixt my soul and God.
I had no power to pass it.   There it sat,
Dark, silent, motionless ; by day and night,

Forever there; shutting me out from God!
But here I see Him, with a tender love,
Beyond all thought, but God's, come nigh to take
My sin away by bearing it Himself;
And with the Cross of Jesus, bridging o'er
The gulf my sin had made.   I am not now,
An outcast and a stranger; self-exiled;
But one with Him who bought me with His blood;
And Life is nothing but the space allowed
To tell of Him to others; and to show
The transformations His great Love can work.
And thus, the Cross shall, ever, stand confessed,
The glory of His Throne.   And when the bands
Of. His Redeemed shall be complete at last,
There shall sound forth, one universal song,
Worthy the Lamb!   For He was slain for us!
And every creature, dwelling on the earth,
And in the far-off worlds shall join the strain,
Glory and Honor, Wisdom, Praise and Power,
To Him that sits upon the Throne of God,
And to the Lamb, forever, evermore!

CANTO THIRD.

THE RESULT.

CANTO III.

ARGUMENT: Jerusalem the night before the Resurrection: Scene at the Tomb: Resurrection of the Lord: Ascension, description of: Effect of: Angels' Announcement to disciples: Pentecost: Tongue of Fire: Church of Christ, what? Thought, concealed from beginning: Description of: Christian and his growth, described: Joy of all things in perfected Redemption: Church goes forth to its work: What opposed to it: Results of its work: Spread and triumph of the Gospel, how accounted for? God's work: Persecution: How met: Prosperity, worse enemy: Constantine, Gospel under: Character of Leaders in Church: God's hidden ones: True greatness defined: Panoramic view of God's Design concerning creation: Sin and Redemption. Truth, spread of: Scientific discoveries, meaning of: Diffusion of error. Future glory of Earth: Coming of Christ for His people: Marriage Supper: Earth: Millennial State: Man's dominion over: What and how obtained: Nations during: Jerusalem: Glory of: Mission among Gentiles: Church of the Resurrection: Season of trial: Christ's Coming in Judgment: Everlasting Age: Great Design complete: Circle traversed, and Results obtained.

86

THE RESULT.

I.

THE Paschal Moon, in full-orbed glory, shone,
In an unclouded sky.   No sound was heard
Above, around, beneath.   Jerusalem
Slept in the moonlight, with as calm a sleep,
As if the guilt of that dread deed of blood
Rested not on it.   On the midnight air,
The hum of the Great City died away;
And silence reigned supreme.   Outside the gates,
The Legionary Guard kept watch, around
The Tomb where Jesus lay ; their measured tread
The only sound that caught the listener's ear.
Slowly, the hours drag on ; when, as the dawn
Begins to tinge the East ; a sudden light
Illumes the sky; an earthquake shakes the ground;
And lo ! an angel of the Lord descends
And rolls away the Stone.   His countenance
Was like the lightning; and his raiment shone
Like snow for brightness.   Overmastering fear
Seized on the soldiers; and they sank to earth,

Appalled and senseless; while the Saviour rose,
And, laying by the garments of the grave,
Looked out upon the world He had redeemed!

II.

By slow degrees, the news that He had risen,
Reached the disciples; and, for forty days,
He mingled with them; ate and drank with them,
And spake about His kingdom.   At the last,
He led them out, as far as Bethany;
And, giving them commission, to proclaim
The everlasting Gospel, till the news
Of His Salvation reached Earth's utmost bounds;
He spake His parting blessing.   As His words
Fell on their ears, what wonder do they see?
Do not their eyes deceive them?   Can it be?
See!   He is rising, with majestic grace,
Against the Law, that holds material forms,
Down to Earth's surface!   Yet, you look in vain,
For outward signs of power.   No rushing wind;
No tempest; no convulsion, marks the scene;
But noiseless as the rising of the Sun,
Is His departure from them.   Wonderingly,
They see His Form receding; and a cloud,
Obedient to His will, bow down to take
The conquering God-Man to His place, once more.
But not alone He went.   Heaven opened wide
Its gates of glorious Light; and angel bands

Sang of His triumph, in responsive notes;
And Cherubim and Seraphim combined
To swell the glory of His train, and yield
A fitting welcome to their Heavenly King.
The everlasting doors lift up their heads,
As angels herald His advancing steps,
Up to the Throne; and heard the Father speak
His joyous greeting, as He took His place
At the right hand of power; and saw His Form
Grow radiant with the splendors that inhered
In His essential Godhead; veiled till then,
Beneath His fleshly dress; now shining out
With the full splendors of Divinity!
O! wondrous vision! Everlasting light
Surrounds the brow, that once, was crowned with
    thorns;
And majesty, with its divinest grace
Enwraps the Form, that hung upon the Cross.
And universal power is in the hands,
That still, retain the wounds which Calvary made.
Jesus stoops down to shame. And lo! that shame
Grows bright with fadeless glory. He endures
Death on the Cross; and forthwith, that becomes
The only gateway to eternal life.
He takes upon Himself the form of Man;
And Man is lifted to the throne of God.
The wounds of Calvary are trophies now;
The Cross, the secret of the Crown. Its blood,
Richer than all Earth's jewels; and His love

8*

His self-forgetful love, the radiant light,
In which His creatures learn to know their God !

I I I.

Deep wonder held them mute.   They stood and
    gazed,
Up to the heavens, as if their eyes once more,
Might rest upon their Lord.   And as they gazed,
A heavenly Messenger drew near and said :
Vainly ye look, ye Men of Galilee !
For this same Jesus shall return no more,
Until that day, when, as ye saw Him go,
He shall again appear !   Then they, with joy,
Sought, once again, the Temple's sacred courts,
While strange emotions moved them ; and their
    song
Was loud and clear, as if a victor's notes
Rang out upon the air.   Must they not speak,
Of their ascended Lord ?   Must they not tell
The glory that surrounds Him ?   They had seen
The Heavens receive Him: and to His dear Name,
They set the music of their thoughts of God !
Then came the Spirit, as a Tongue of Fire ;
Symbol of the new ministry, whose work
Was proclamation of the Saviour's name,
Man's speech; God's power to vitalize that speech!
God's Truth ; Man's utterance. If the Tongue of
    Fire

Attests that truth, the simplest words we speak,
Will glow and corruscate with light divine ;
Or lie upon the spirit, like the dew
Upon the tender herb ; or thrill the soul
With a new power of life.   The Priesthood, now,
Gives place to other ministry ; in which,
The Word of Truth is the sole instrument ;
The Holy Ghost the Witness : and the Cross,
The Centre of attraction.   There is now,
No Altar, Priest or Sacrifice, but Christ.
And where the Tongue of Fire attests His work,
The Living Church is found — but nowhere else.

IV.

What is that Church ?   Prophets had told of it,
In phrase obscure ; but never had the thought
Dawned on the minds of men, until the race,
Chosen of God to witness to His Truth,
Proved faithless to its trust.   His Spirit, then,
Gave utterance to it, as the Thought of God,
From everlasting ; and the sons of men
Saw its dim outline, faintly at the first,
But growing in its beauty, as it took
The clearer lines and more engaging hues,
Of the fair vision, as it always stood,
A living fact before Jehovah's eye !
What is that Church ?   A people, formed to be
His own peculiar treasure.   To no Sect,

No Creed, no Nationality, confined ;
It numbers all, who own the Name of Christ,
The Rock on which they build ; and find His love,
The power of separation from their sins.
By His convincing power, the Holy Ghost
Attests the Word ; and as, beneath the deep,
O'er which He brooded, a new world was formed ;
So, 'neath the darkness of our lost estate,
The spirit's new creation is achieved,
And Christ is formed within. The new-born soul
Emerges from the darkness ; and in light,
Attests its heavenly birth. It spreads its wings
Of Faith and Hope, in the new atmosphere
Of Christ's constraining Love. Faintly at first,
And with a tremulous motion, it attempts
The exercise of Faith ; as if in fear
Of its own act. But, increase of the power
Comes from its use. And, as the unfledged bird
Grows into plumage ; and the power of song
Takes on development, until he stands,
Acknowledged in the fulness of its life :
So grows the Christian in his life of faith.
The nest first claims him in his callow state :
Where oft, unconsciously, his wing is stretched
As if in prophecy of coming flight !
But *will* it come ? Can faith, as weak as his,
Grow as in others ? Yes : but exercise
Of what he has, must be its law of growth.
And soon from this, the sense of freedom comes,

As growing power springs up from active use.
Then comes occasion ; and the voice within,
Answers the call without. He spreads his wings ;
He mounts ; he soars ; rejoicing in the sense
Of new-born liberty ; and ere he knows,
The song of triumph gushes, sweetly, forth !
And thus all growth is perfected. Each step
Becomes a platform, whence we learn to mount,
Up to the next above. And as the plant
Grows up from immaturity, and blooms
Into the liberty of Bud and Flower ;
So *he* matures, from the first act of faith,
Into the inflorescence of a soul
That blooms for God alone. Henceforth for him,
There is no music with so sweet a sound,
As that of Jesus' Name : no portion, like
The treasures of His Love ; no liberty
So perfect as the freedom of His Law :
No service like His work ; and no reward
So glorious as the knowledge of Himself!
He lives and moves in this. His spirit's choice
Turns to it, with a tremulous delight,
And seeks for nought beyond. For Heaven itself,
Is just where He unveils Himself to souls,
That share in His great love. And they who know
Its fulness and its meaning, own in Him,
The measure of all fulness ; and the pledge,
That every blessing stands secure in Him !
The soul's fresh springs are found in Him, alone ;

And as they flow in blessings down to us,
They sparkle in the sunlight of His smile.
And Life's best harmonies are but the sound
Of His salvation, in the souls of men.
These make His Church; and these, in every land,
He now is gathering.   They shall come at last,
From every nation, kindred, tribe and tongue;
And in Earth's new Creation, take the place
Of highest power and station.   For no Creed,
Known upon earth, can trace the only path
By which lost souls may seek and find their God.
The gathering of the people is *to Him:*
And He has access, by unnumbered ways,
To those who seek His face.   His truth can come,
In forms we know not of, to ruined souls,
And save them from their ruin ; though the tongue
May not be able, into forms of speech,
To syllable the trust that moves within.
His precious blood may prove a saving power,
Where our Theology ignores the work,
Not fashioned by its rules.   And at the last,
From Earth's remotest bounds, they shall come forth
First in His kingdom, whom *we* proudly thought,
Excluded from it ; while no place is found
For those, who deemed themselves the foremost
          there !
These make His Church : the glory and the crown
Of His Creation ; showing forth to men
God's Image, reproduced in human souls ;

His Likeness made incarnate ; shining out,
In men whom Sin had ruined, and His Love
Had rescued from their Sin.   And when at last,
That Church shall stand complete ; when God's
     Great Thought
Shall be incorporate in History ;
The Harp of Nature shall awake the strain
Of exultation in the general joy
Of Man, redeemed from Sin.   O ! nevermore
Shall notes of discord issue from its strings !
Its soul of harmony is perfect, now .
As the great thought of God's Redeeming Love,
Illumines all His works ; and finds itself,
In countless echoes speaking forth His praise !
The Shepherd will have brought the wandering
     sheep
Of this revolted Earth, back to its place,
Amid the sisterhood of worlds — no more
A wanderer from the fold ; but ever known
By the strange contrasts of its history ;
Of Sin, and of Redemption from its power.
Of Sin, a burden on the heart of God ;
And God becoming Man, that on the Cross,
He might bring in Redemption for the race,
That sold itself in slavery unto Sin !

V.

And now the Church goes forth to do its work,
With the new Gospel of The Nazarene

Arrayed against it, were the Purse and Sword,
The Learning, Laws and Genius of the World.
An Idol Worship ruled in every land:
Kings were its priests; and Princes strove to be
Its honored servitors.   The Laws were made,
To guard its altars.   Eloquence attained
Its loftiest flights, in bringing it renown,
And Poets garlanded immortal songs,
In praises of its gods.   It spake: and lo!   ,
The World bowed down in homage to its will.
This on the one side.   On the other — what?
A band of men, unlearned; and ignorant
Of all the graces, which the Schools could teach.
They could not weave, with dialectic skill,
The subtle theories, which engrossed the minds
Of Poets and Philosophers: or rouse
The admiration of the listening throng,
By their commanding eloquence.   No power,
Honor or state was theirs.   They could not touch
One spring of influence, which the nations held
In honor, love or fear.   They stood alone:
The weakest of the weak: Their daily toil
Their means of daily bread.   And yet these men,
With nothing but the story of the Cross,
O'erthrew these altars: turned aside the feet,
Of those who sought them, to the simple rites
Of the New Worship: Into daily life,
Brought the new factors, Faith and Hope and
      Love;

Taught men forgiveness of the deadliest wrongs
For His dear sake, who bought us with His blood.
Proclaimed the body's sanctity as meant
To be the Temple of the Living God;
And therefore to be honored, and kept free
From outward filthiness or inward stain :
Inspired contempt of death, by the new hope
Of resurrection : showed men how, to live,
A life of cheerful, self-renouncing love
Fearful of nought but sin ; and passed the bonds
Of common brotherhood around our race,
In the humanity of Jesus Christ !

VI.

How shall we read this problem ?   How assign
A cause sufficient for these vast results ?
Man's power avails not here.   He could as soon,
Restore the dead to life, as wake the thrill
Of an immortal hope, in human souls.
And, as the question presses for reply,
The answer comes, It was the power of God,
In the new Gospel of the Crucified
That wrought these triumphs !   Kings and Con-
    querors,
Have left no record that can equal this.
The Fishermen of Galilee eclipse
In their achievements, all the brightest deeds
Of those whom men call great.   And then, to test

9   G

The strength of their foundation, storms arose :
And Persecution came, and robed itself ·
In all the terrors of the Sword and Stake.
The Rack assumed its deadliest device,
Of mortal agony ; and Prison-gloom   ·
Sunk to its deepest depths to shake the soul,
From its fidelity of trust in God !
No age was spared.   Matron and blooming maid ;
Youth in its flush of manly strength: old age,
In its decrepitude : and infancy,
In the first sunlight of its opening life :
Went down before the terrors of the storm !
Ten times the fires of persecution raged ; *
Ten times Imperial Power arrayed itself,
In garments, rolled in blood, to hunt the name
Of Christian from the earth.   Ten times, the strife
Seemed to defy Satanic skill, to find
More subtle mode of torture.   Yet in each,
The Faith that looked to Jesus and His Cross,
Was more than conqueror ; and triumphed still,
In its calm words of Confidence in Him.   ·
And still they grew ; and still the wonder spread

---

* I do not wish to be understood as meaning that this is the
number of the Persecutions.   For as Dr. Schaff rightly ob-
serves, "This number is, in any view, incorrect ; too great for
the general persecutions ; and far too small for the provincial
and local."—*Hist. of Christ. Ch.*, p. 161.

I suppose it is quite allowable, thus to set forth a large but
indefinite number ?   ·

Of Persecution mowing down their ranks,
Which still grew up again; * and in each growth,
Produced again that purity of life;
That simple trust in Jesus; and that love
To all who bore His name, that turned the eyes
Of all mankind upon them, and drew forth
The praise of those who hunted them to death!

. VII.

But now a new and deadlier danger rose. ·
The old arbitrament of Fire and Sword
Failed of its end.   For Truth is Victor, still,
E'en when it seems the vanquished.   Has it not,
A heavenly birth, and resurrection-power?
It, therefore, cannot die.   Forth from each grave,
Where men attempt its burial, it springs
With all the fulness of immortal life.
And thus, the Gospel, from these bloody fields,
Went forth to fresh encounters.   Outward foes
Gave place to other enemies, who waged
Warfare more dangerous, than the brutal one
Of Fire and Sword; and with consummate skill,
Wielded the weapons of luxurious ease.
The Roman Constantine took the new Faith,

---

* "All your refinements of cruelty can accomplish nothing :
on the contrary, they serve as a lure to this sect. *Our number increases the more you destroy us.* The blood of the
Christians is the seed of a new harvest." —*Tertullian in Apol.*

Into his keeping ; marking out its path,
Through flowery fields ; and gayly wreathed the
     Cross,
With the rewards of office.   Men bowed down,
Before that Symbol, when Imperial hands
Held it aloft ; or when they saw it wave,
On Cæsar's banners, o'er his conquering hosts ;
That would have hunted to a bloody death,
Its unprotected followers.   Thousands took
The Name of Jesus on their lips, who knew
Nothing of His great love ; and saw, in it,
Nought but the path of honor in the State.
And others stepped into the Stream of Life
Only to foul its waters.   Errors spread
In wild profusion : and the Church of Christ
Seemed rent asunder, with the strife of those
Who claimed to guard its truth : but taught, instead,
Wild fancies of their own.   Hypocrisy *
Upreared its head : and with unblushing front,
Professed the faith it neither knew nor loved.
Yet still the Truth remained.   Its inward Life
Which proved victorious over Fire and Sword ;
Conquered the blandishments of Power and State.
Its Standard-Bearers might betray their trust ;

* "Even Eusebius, the panegyrist of Constantine . . . .
even he is obliged to reckon among the grievous evils of this
period, of which he was an eye-witness, the *indescribable hypocrisy* of those who gave themselves out as Christians merely
for temporal advantage."—*Neander's Hist.*, vol. ii., p. 28.

Or fall in its defence : but other hands
Would wave it still, aloft, till every breeze
Made dalliance with its folds ; and every land
Heard of the Gospel of the Grace of God!
Thus, every form of danger brought to light,
Men of that giant stature, that could stand
Conspicuous 'midst a host; and draw around
Their single selves, the interest of the fight.
They came to Jesus, as his warriors came
To David at Adullam — in distress ;
Borne down with debt, and weary of the yoke
Of service thus far borne. And in their need,
He took them to Himself; broke off their bonds ;
Breathed a new life within ; and for the fight,
Trained them around the Cross. And thus they
    grew,
From weakness into strength ; and took their place
As Leaders in the host. Did dangers press ?
They rallied to the front. Did Duty speak ?
They heard her voice, and gladly gave themselves
Responsive to her call. No foe was deemed,
Too strong for them to combat ; and no lamb
In all the flock, too weak for them to feed.
Nothing was little, if it only touched
The interests of His work ; and nothing great,
Save as it stood connected with His Cause!
These were the Leaders. But, amid the hosts,
Thousands were found, whose names—tho' never
    traced,

9 *

Upon the scroll of History; and known
Only among the lowliest — told of lives,
Made beautiful by Faith and Hope and Love.
They moved as benedictions among men ;
Revealed, as violets in the grassy fields,
By the sweet perfume which they breathe around !
With stronger self-assertion, they might well
Have won the place of honor in the church,
Or stood as leaders in it : but they chose
The lowlier sphere of self-forgetful love,
Enough for them if, in the Master's eye,
Their work stood forth approved. Enough if they
But won His loving smile, or heard at last,
His lips pronounce, *Thou faithful one, well done !*

VIII.

And thus the Cause of Christ went round the world,
Dispensing blessings, as the Spring does flowers.
Oppression could not strangle it : nor wealth,
With its allurements, wean men from their hold
Of simple trust in God. There was no might,
In all that Man could do, to break the power
That held them in allegiance to His Name.   '
He who has seen the Sun can ne'er forget
Its light and splendor. And when on the soul
Jesus arises, Sun-like, in the light
Of His great love ; in vain, you seek to fill
The measure of its needs, with aught that stops

Short of Himself. The soul has found its God!
Men talk of greatness, as if aught were great,
That makes itself the Centre; or that works
For its own ends. No. In the Master's Life,
We read the secret. He, alone is great,
Who can forget himself; and take the place
Of servitude; if thus he may become
A power in living souls, to lift them up,
Out of their sin to Life and Purity.
Service is Honor when its spring is Love.
And Love is noblest, when it gives itself,
In sacrifice for those who, else were lost.
Men seem divine, when they forget themselves,
And live for others' good. And thus it comes
That in Life's lowliest walks, we meet with those
Who well could grace the highest; and who spread
O'er all things round, the sweet attractiveness
Of Labor for His Name. It matters not,
That men o'erlooked them, in their estimate
Of Life's controlling forces. None the less
Their influence comes as comes the Stellar Light,
Mingling with that of Day. You see it not;
You know not that you feel it; yet it makes
An estimated portion of the sum
Of the World's Light: and mingles with the Heat,
That keeps the springs of Life, in constant play!

IX.

Here then we linger.   As God's Great Design
Became incarnate in The Christ, so all
Its great results shall centre still in Him.
And as its waves of blessedness roll on,
He shall be found the Light of every joy:
The Source of every blessing: and the Spring
Whence issues full salvation for the world!
Jesus is in the centre; and His smile
Bears light and life to everything that lives.
I look and see God's Purpose for the Earth,
Established on it, as a living fact
As I look on through Him.   In Him, it takes
Objective form, and robes itself about
In human history, as it always was
In God's conception of it.   First, it comes
In Eden's beauty, smiling on us there,
As from the womb of Night, the earth came forth;
And Life before unknown — Grass, Herb and
      Flower —
Sprang into being, and exhaled their sweets,
And sparkled in the jewelry of morn.
Bird, Beast, Fish, Insect, in unnumbered forms,
Next heard His voice; and answering, made the
      Earth,
The Air, the Ocean, redolent with joy.
Last, Man appeared: and took his station there,
The Image and the Likeness of his God:

There were no discords, in Earth's Birth-Day Song:
No notes but those of Peace and Joy and Love!
But Sin came next; and yet its fearful shock
Jarred not that Purpose from its equipoise,
Or turned it from its course. It held its way,
As calmly as the Sun, when tempest-clouds
Obscure its light; and with its force divine,
Works thro' the darkness, till the clouds disperse,
And leave the face of heaven in smiles, once more!
So God held on the counsel of His Grace,
Unchanged, unchanging. And when *He* came forth,
In Whom that counsel was to be fulfilled;
And men, rejecting, nailed Him to the Cross,
And laid Him in the Tomb, no outward sign
Told of approaching wrath. The Sun arose,
As calmly as before. The Moon looked down,
Upon His guarded Tomb, as peacefully
As if that deed were worthy of its light.
All things went on in their accustomed course;
And when He rose, the Conqueror of Death,
No Victor's shout awoke the slumbering world,
With the loud voice of triumph. From their midst,
Men saw a feeble band, weak and unlearned,
Go forth to tell of Jesus and His Cross,
And triumph in His victory o'er the Grave.
And still, to-day, that story is renewed;
And blooming maids; and young men in their
    strength;
And hoary-headed sires: and lisping babes;

Men crowned with knowledge, and maturely wise;
Or ignorant of all things, save the course
Of each day's common duties, own His Name,
The Source of all their blessings; and His Love,
The secret Spring of the best joys they know.
In radiant glory, through the heavens of Thought;
He moves, full-orbed; and every sparkling wave,
Rising and falling on the Sea of Life,
Bears witness to His power. And still it spreads;
And Science lays her tribute at His feet,
Who is Himself, the Truth: and in each field
Of her extending triumphs, brings to light,
New tokens of His Wisdom and His Power.
Unconsciously, she brings them: knowing not
That the resplendent coronet she frames,
Shall sparkle with His Name, in every gem.
Therefore I bid those toilers, in the mine
Of Nature's wealth, God-speed in their great work!
I own them all co-workers for the Truth,
As far as *Truth* is gained.   I thrill beneath
The hopes which they inspire: and look beyond,
To hail the coming of a brighter day,
Whose intimations greet me, in the view
Of their achievements.   What if some despond?
I cannot tremble for the Ark of God;
Or fear for the foundation of His Word!
I know Whose arm sustains it, though unseen.
Nothing but Error perishes.   The Truth,
Whate'er its name, remains.   Allied to God,

As sunbeams to the Sun, it holds its way
Untouched by change, and smiling at the storm.
I know Whose will pervades the wondrous facts,
Which Science brings to light ; and knowing this,
I look with strong expectancy, to see
Its fields extending ; and, with joyous heart,
Its varied triumphs hail ! They are to me,
More than the work of Law : for, in them all
I trace my Father's hand, Who shows me thus,
What thoughts of beauty have their home in Him
And still, I look to see these wonders spread.
For, everywhere, new triumphs wait their birth,
Into our knowledge. New disclosures stand
Waiting the hour that brings them into view ;
And seem, in their expectancy, to chide
The dulness of our vision, that so long
Was closed against them ; tho' their beauty forms
A portion of Earth's dowry from her God.

X.

And side by side with this, the Truth that tells
Of Jesus and His Cross, shall still, go on
Winning new triumphs ; in the hearts of men,
Quick'ning new hopes ; inspiring new desires ;
And teaching, how a child-like faith in Him,
Can build our Manhood's best proportions up.
But, with each effort to extend the Truth,
Falsehood shall coin its counterfeited lie.

Thought shall be free ! but thousands shall mistake
License for Freedom, and drift far away,
From the old moorings of the Word of God,
To find their freedom, servitude to self.
And Wickedness shall spread ; and take new forms
To suit the changing aspects of the times ;
Until at last, the promised end draws nigh,
And Earth looks up, in her Millennial Dawn.
But not by slow development, it comes ?
For, as the Sun arising, brings the day ;
So Christ, the Sun of Righteousness, must rise
On the astonished earth, ere it can see
The morn of its long-promised Day of Rest.
And, as the Telescope brings worlds unseen,
Within our scope of vision : so I look
Through the Prophetic Word, and see beyond,
Its promised glories ripened into fact.
The Hope of all His Church ; the long Desired
Of every nation, has appeared at last !
He comes to reap the Harvest, from the seed,
Scattered for ages ; and to bring the sheaves,
Into the garner of The Father's House !
His waiting Church is gathered to Himself:
Their sleeping dust has started into life ;
The living saints are changed ; and both, arrayed
In bodies like His own, are taken up
To meet Him in the air : and swell the joy,
That crowns the Marriage Supper of the Lamb !

XI.

I may not speak of *that*. For who can paint,
In human speech, the wonders of that scene?
No! We must lay aside this mortal dress,
And robe ourselves in immortality;
Ere we can tell its meaning. For we know
What we experience, only. All beyond:
All that will *be* experience, when we wear
Our resurrection-bodies, lies within
The realm of Hope — above our knowledge now.
O! the transcendent glories of the scene,
That rises on my sight, as I survey
This panoramic vision of His Word!
For, with His chosen, at the Marriage-Feast,
Jesus comes forth to smite the Man of Sin;
And overthrow his works; and rid the Earth
Of his polluting presence! From that hour,
Sin rules the world no more. Its wintry storms
Give place to Spring-time blessedness; and Peace
Sits brooding, dove-like, o'er its troubled waves,
Tossed with the tempests of six thousand years!
The Sabbath of the World has come, at last;
And all things whisper of its quiet rest!

XII.

In Types and Symbols, was this Vision sketched
In the Prophetic Word. And men looked on,

10

And as the ages passed, in wonder asked,
What mean these Types?   And now, the answer
    comes
As from the bud comes forth the perfect flower.
The nations are at rest.   The shock of war
Is heard no more among them.   For when *He*
Assumes His coronet as Prince of Peace,
All things bear witness to it.   Nature thrills,
With the deep harmony His presence breathes
Thro' all His works.   The Curse has lost its power;
And barrenness afflicts the earth no more.
Ungrudgingly, it pours its treasures forth;
Nor claims the hard expenditure of toil,
Before it yields its treasures.   In the ear
Of him who gathers in the golden grain,
The ploughman's song sounds merrily.   The plants,
That now, begirt with armature of thorns,
Their flower or fruit, yield to their primal law
A prompt obedience; and instead of thorns,
Their fuller life unfolds the perfect leaf,
Or forms the opening flower.   The wilderness
Smiles out with joy; and henceforth like the rose,
The desert blossoms, and the mountain's brow
Waves like old Lebanon, when Summer winds
Made music with its cedars.   Living streams
Gush out in sandy deserts; and the flow
Of rippling waters, fills the air with song.
The gentle poise between opposing powers,
That ruled the air, before the tempest's shock,

Spread round the earth a purer atmosphere,
Has sway once more. Health laughs in every
    breeze,
Though storms convulse and Tempests rage no
    more.
The Earth, restored to its primeval state,
Rejoices in the fuller life, that first,
Bore sway upon its surface. All its tribes
Share in the glorious liberty, decreed
The sons of God; and in one burst of joy,
Roll round the Earth, Creation's song of praise.
The hour of its long travail comes at last;
And Nature, now is born! Its powers, repressed
Through the past ages, burst at last, to life:
And whatsoe'er its processes have told
Of hidden beauty; of unconscious powers;
And capabilities, scarce dreamed of yet,
Start into being, and attest the wealth
Of the rich heritage, at first bestowed.

XIII.

And o'er this scene of beauty, Man walks forth
With absolute dominion. In his hands,
He holds the reins of power, as at the first;
And all things own him lord. Harmoniously,
Without a thought of harm, or sense of fear,
They move around him : owning the control,
Which his obedience to the Will of God,

Makes absolute o'er them.   I see at last,
What our humanity in Jesus Christ,
Makes perfect Manhood mean ; and in His work,
Behold that lost humanity restored !
The secret things which Science brings to light ;
With slow and patient toil, become at once,
His, as by intuition.   For the mind
In harmony with God, perceives the truth
Embodied in His works, much as the eye
Detects the light ; and passes at one bound,
To knowledge of the process and result.
And is not this dominion ?   Was not this,
Man's heritage at first ?   If it was lost
By sin and folly : If he sought to gain
By his own power, the headship over all ;
Six thousand years of toil and care and pain,
Have taught him what he needs ; and now he stands
Throned in the work of Jesus, and receives
Through Him his lost inheritance.   The crown
Is Man's, once more ; but all its glory tells
Of His dear Name, who saved us by His blood.
All things are full of Him.   The nations learn
The story of His love : and find therein
A new-creating power.   His Truth distils
Gently, as showers upon the tender herb :
And spreads new life ; and in the souls of men,
Kindles new hopes, and wakens new desires ;
And builds up perfect manhood, on the type
Of character in Jesus.   All that tempts

To sin and violence, is put away;
And Righteousness takes up its home on earth,
And rules among the nations. He comes forth
The Rod from Jesse's stem; the Righteous Branch
Out of his roots ; and calmly, 'neath His shade,
The nations find repose. Upon Him rests
The Spirit of the Lord ; and twines the wreath
Of radiant glory, in that wondrous Name,
Which speaks His nature, to the hearts of men !
The Wonderful, the Secret ; Counsellor ;
The Everlasting Father ; Mighty God ;
The Prince of Peace—What can be added here?
His is the Name of blessing ; calling forth
Life's sweetest music in the souls of men :
And human enterprise flows, freely, forth
Beneath its sheltering power : and everywhere,
All Nature smiles in harmony with Him !
The King has come at last! The shout that hails
His glorious Advent thrills the world with life
And wakes it to a joy before unknown !

XIV.

The nations hear, and own the claim divine, ·
He makes to their allegiance. Is He not,
The World's Redeemer ? Is He not the One
Whom, thro' the ages, men have waited for,
While yet they knew Him not? And now He comes,
And all things hail His coming. In the light

10 *   II

Of His appearing, darkness flees away;
And Peace and Joy walk forth upon the earth.
The lesson of one blood is learned at last; .
And men, rejoicing, feel the sacred tie,
Of Fatherhood in God, in His dear Name,
Who makes them one in Him.   Jerusalem
Sits in the place of honor.   From afar,
The Gentiles see her rising; and their kings
Bring of their glory to her.   She becomes
A name of praise and power upon the earth;
A diadem of beauty in the hands
Of her Redeeming God.   Her sons stand forth,
His chosen witnesses; and tell abroad
The story of His acts in their behalf.
For ages, they had gone around the earth
A living Miracle, attesting still,
Although unconsciously, His Word of Truth,
Which, through the desolations of the past,
Kept guard around them; holding them in life,
When nations, mightier far had passed away!
And now the veil is lifted.   As they look,
Lo! The true Joseph stands revealed at last!
O! the deep wonder of that gracious hour!
The darkness passes.   Light, within their souls,
Rises in full-orbed glory; and they see
The meaning of that wondrous Life and Death
By which He sought to win them to Himself.
Was ever love like His?   Was ever guilt
As crimson-dyed as theirs?   Yet, He forgives!

And with the sense of pardon, they awake,
And thrill with the new life His Love begets.
Henceforth, they live, but to show forth His praise,
And speak of Him to others.   And *they* hear
Of His transforming grace, who through the past,
Had lived in utter darkness ; bowing down
To gods their hands had made. And when they hear,
They own Him Sovereign Lord; the unknown One
Whom, in their ignorance, they robed about,
With passions like their own. To Him they bow ;
And bring the perfume of adoring hearts,
When first they hear His Name. And thus, the seed
Of Abraham become, as prophets said,
The world's instructors ; showing forth His praise ;
And scattering blessings round a ransomed world.
His glorious attributes burst into view
In passing through their history, as Light
Breaks into rainbows, when it meets a cloud.
And Israel, circled thus, as in a bow
Of iridescent glory stands confessed,
First of the nations ; bringing Light and Life,
To those' who sat in Darkness and in Death.

XV.

But not alone they labor.   By their side,
Robed in the garments of immortal Life,
The Children of the Resurrection stand ;
And in their heavenly ministry, proclaim

The riches of His Grace. Girt round with power,
They know no weakness : feel no touch of sin ;
And dream of death, no more. What spirit prompts
Their bodies execute ; as free as it
To move unfettered through the realms of space.
For what is this, but the inheritance
That waits our fuller life?   The mastery
Of sinless beings o'er Creation's laws,
By harmony with Him Whose will they speak ?
No weariness attends their service now.
Does spirit weary?   And the form that owns
Affinity with spirit, feels the thrill
Of an undying life in all its powers.
No pain can touch them ; no disease invade ;
No languor enervate : no labor tire.
The Lamb, amidst the Throne, shall lead them forth
Beside the living waters.   They shall feel
Hunger and thirst no more. His hand shall wipe
All tears, from every eye ; and all the ills
Of their experience, in this mortal state,
Shall pass like troubled dreams.   And thus they
      move,
In radiant glory 'midst the sons of men,
As angels did at first.   Familiarly,
They tell the story of the Saviour's love ;
And in themselves, best illustrate its power.
Its germ blooms out, in everlasting life ;
And all the glory of their deathless state
Is but its ripened fruit.   To other worlds,

They bear the wondrous tidings ; and proclaim
In all the mansions of the Father's House
The riches of His grace, who gave Himself
A Sacrifice to take away their sin ;
And bring the wanderer back again to God.
The Patriarch's Dream is realized, at last ;
And angels pass, in loving intercourse,
Between the Heavens and Earth — too long
    estranged —
Upon the Ladder of His Finished Work !
And now He wears the Crown. To Him of right,
Alone belongs its glory; for the Cross,
When rightly understood, is Victory
In its sublimest forms. The Crown, the Throne,
Is but its due result : and all the power,
That sways the sceptre of His Government,
And leads the soul a captive to its God,
Is but the issue of Incarnate Love ;
And had its birth, as certain consequence,
In His Self-Sacrifice for guilty men.
From Earth's remotest bounds, one song goes up
Of praise to His great Name. The old man tells,
In trembling speech, its preciousness and power ;
And sighing, reckons it Life's greatest loss
That its best days were spent, in ignorance
That veiled Him from his view. In the warm flush
Of manly strength, the Youth recounts His praise ;
The maiden joins the strain ; while Infancy,
In its sweet accents, whispers of the Love,

That gave the world the Babe of Bethlehem !
All states of life ; all characters ; combine
To swell the song, that, through Creation rolls
A ransomed World's just tribute to His praise.

X V I.

I sing not of the Trial, that breaks in
Upon these scenes of blessedness : nor tell
How the Arch-Tempter is let loose again,
To try his cunning snares ; and test the strength
Of what appeared to be new life within.
Is it a Life ?   And will it *choose* the Good ?
Can Evil take it, in its cunning snares ?
Or will its inward Sense of Right detect
The subtle lie ?   Can strong assault break down
The arm of its defence ?   Or will it stand,
In fearless conflict for the Right and True ?
This must be proved—for less than this, would be
To build upon the sand.   Ere we can see
The Everlasting Age, upon the Earth ;
Man must be rooted, in the choice of Good,
For its own sake : and yield responsive notes
To all the Will of God.   Thus Trial comes
Upon the Earth once more ; and nations feel
The shock of contest, 'twixt the Good and Ill.
I sing not of this now : but pass beyond
To the transcendent glories of the scene,
In which the Harvest of the Earth is reaped,

And all things that offend are put away
From the Redeemer's Kingdom. He reserves
This triumph to Himself; and gloriously,
His own right arm achieves the victory!
Heaven opens wide its glorious gates, as He,
Throned in the clouds, in majesty divine,
With His attendant angels, swelling wide
The splendors of His train, comes down to Earth.
The Great White Throne is set; and from His face,
The Earth and Heavens in wonder, flee away!
For, is not He, the Incarnate Love of God?
And what can blaze, with such consuming fire,
As Perfect Love; when it has passed the bounds
Of its divine forbearance? Is not Light,
Whose sweetest smile is Heaven's unclouded blue,
One with its fiery crimson? Is not that,
Unseen, electric force, whose gentle touch
Opens the Evening Primrose, with a start,
One with the lightning-flash that blasts the Oak?
And that deep, tender, everlasting Love,
Which led Him to the Cross: and moved the springs,
Of all its tender ministries, is yet,
One, in its essence, with that fiery Wrath,
That burns against incorrigible Ill!
Thus, on His Judgment-Throne as on His Cross,
Love rules in all He does. It rears the Throne;
Surrounds it with its splendors; and declares,
The Sentence, that shall purge the World from sin,
And separate the evil from the good!

But of that sentence who may dare to speak?
When He Whose lips pronounce it, draws the veil
Of outer darkness round it?   He alone,
Knows its full meaning.   God forbid, that I
Should seek to lift that veil ; or paint the scene,
That lies concealed, behind it !   Death is there,
Because *He* is not !   But what Death may be,
In this conception of it — who can tell ?
This much we know: In the Revealing Day,
He will disclose it: and the Heavens shall shout,
And Earth, rejoicing, echo back the strain
Judgment and Righteousness support His Throne!

XVII.

And now the vision that has struggled long,
Amid surrounding darkness, dissipates
The clouds that overhung it.   What a scene
Of radiant glory, bursts upon the sight !
Earth stands revealed, as angels saw it once,
In its first bloom of beauty.   All that tells
Of blight and barrenness, disease and death,
Is put away forever.   From above,
The Sun looks down, with life-imparting beams ;
And draws no pestilence from reeking soils,
Charged with the germs of death ; nor, with its heat,
Scorches the tender plant.   The Moon and Stars
Shed their serenest glory ; for their light
Streams through an atmosphere that yields it all,

To human view ; yet, so entrancingly
Spreads its delicious influence, that to breathe,
Is to receive the impulse of new life.
In all its borders, Earth has now, become
Man's fitting Habitation. Fiery heat,
And deadly cold, are known on it no more.
While all that fosters all the powers of Life
And brings them forth in full development,
Is found upon it ; and it stands confessed
Worthy His Thought, Who made it thus at first ;
Worthy His Love, Who ransomed it when lost ;
Worthy His Purpose, Who through all the gloom
And desolation of Man's dark revolt,
Meant to restore it ; and has now, achieved
This part of the great counsel of His Grace !
Sing of its restoration, Ye who dwell
In the surrounding planets ! Open wide
Your heavenly gates, Ye Sisterhood of Worlds,
To let the Wanderer in ! Nor deem the place
Of precedence, in all your glorious hosts,
Too high for her, who bears upon her brow,
The Coronet of God's Redeeming Love !
The Kingdom is the Lord's ; and all that makes,
Serenest harmony and perfect bliss,
Is centred in its bounds. One language serves
Through all its borders ; and from every tribe,
Near and remote, is heard one common strain
Of glory to His Name ; and every heart
Offers its love, and every voice its praise.

11

See! how Heaven opens; and the shining throngs
Of Resurrection-Saints press down to greet,
And mingle with the Brotherhood of Earth!
What glory crowns each brow! What radiant light,
With its sweet halo, circles every form!
They need no Sun by day, nor Moon by night;
For God's essential glory drives away
All darkness where they dwell; and in its beams
The nations walk secure. The Throne of God
And of the Lamb is there; and out of it,
The Stream of Life, with its mellifluous flow,
Sends forth its crystal waters, on whose brink
The Tree of Life unfolds its healing leaves,
And yields its precious fruit. The Flaming Sword,
No longer guards it now: the Cherubim
Protect its fruit no more: but angel hands
Dispense it to the nations, and they eat,
And, in the flush of its Immortal Life,
Become superior to the touch of Death.
There *is* no Death. It disappears with Sin:
And all the ills that follow in its train,
Cease, like the shadow, when the substance fails!
In Earth: in Heaven: and in the far-off worlds,
God's Will is done, and prompt obedience rules
Each thought of Man; each interest of his life;
And all the combinations that affect
Surrounding nations, and the lower tribes
That dwell in peace about him. All, alike,
Proclaim how perfectly that Will is done;

And how it moves, in harmony divine,
Through Nature's deepest workings. God's Great
    Thought,
Circling the Universe, comes back to Earth;
And in the sweep and glory of its work,
Finds Man redeemed, and purified from Sin:
The Evil banished, to return no more;
And God Himself, revealed through Jesus Christ,
The All in all; Supreme and Perfect Good!

MISCELLANEOUS POEMS.

MISCELLANEOUS POEMS.

THE STORY OF LITTLE THINGS.

" There are more things in Heaven and Earth, Horatio,
Than are dreamed of in your philosophy."

I.

A LITTLE One sat on her Grandpa's knee,
  And her curls fell gracefully on his breast;
While she sought with a burst of childlike glee,
  To pillow her head on that place of rest.
He was old and withered; if we
  Might judge from the lines upon his face.
Old and withered and worn; while she
  Was fresh as light in its morning grace.
Was he indeed, so? Do you think,
That Life can be known, while on its brink,
We tread, with the free and gladsome airs,
That Childhood, in its freshness wears?
I know there are notes which *it* can touch,
Clear and sweet and ringing: but much

That makes Life's grandest harmony,
Is to it unknown. For we
Must range the Octaves o'er and o'er,
  The tenor of joy, and the bass of pain ;
And blend their varying notes, before
  We learn the compass of the strain,
  Or join in the swell of its full refrain.
We may grow young, as years increase ;
  And brighter thoughts than Childhood guessed,
May spring from the hoary head, when Peace
  Has made its home in the aged breast.
Fancy may move with its lightest grace ;
  And Hope with its most elastic tread ;
And Love of the Beautiful hold its place,
  In hearts, whose dearest hopes are fled ;
When we come to learn, that Life may be,
Only the Bud of Eternity ;
Waiting here for the Spring to come,
When it blossoms out in its Heavenly Home !

II.

"Tell me a story," — the Little One said.
  And the Old Man looked, with a bright'ning
    eye,
As he laid his hand on her curly head,
  And thus, to his darling, made reply.
"A Story, Little One ! What shall it be ?"
  "A real, live story, Grandpa, please ;

Of the Little Folks, we cannot see,
  Who dance in the Rain-drops and sing in the
    Trees,
When the Wind is blowing, merrily —
For you said there *were* such, once, you know."

"Yes! my Darling! Long ages ago ;
Long before Grandpa himself was born ;
Long before *his* first saw the morn ;
Or his, or his, in a length'ning line —
Men had strange thoughts of the Power Divine :
And peopled the Earth, Woods, Air and Springs,
With countless hosts of Little Things,
People we ought to call them : who, —
Pervading Nature, through and through —
Had forms so tiny that they could sup,
In the dainty folds of the Butter-Cup ;
Or hide themselves, till Evening's close,
In the spiral forms of the sweet Primrose
And then, with a sudden burst and shout,
Let its delicious fragrance, out !
They could ride on the wave in a Muscle-Shell,
  As the Moonbeams glanced on the glistening tide ;
And feel their Fairy bosoms swell
  With the thrilling touch of Elfin pride.
They had all hours beneath their sway ;
But better far than the garish day,
They loved the quiet hours of night,
When all things slept in the pale moonlight ;

I

And the busy world was hushed and still ;
  And nought was heard but the watch-dog's
    bark,
As he bayed the Moon from the distant hill ;
  And the owl was hooting in forests dark.
Then, roused by the stroke of the Wood-tick's
    Clock,
  As he kept the hours in the haunted Oak ;
They would spring from their homes in the rifted
    rock,
  And answer the call, which his summons spoke.
Away, away, they would speed them on,
Ere the wizard hours of night were gone !
Some, from the Glens and the Caves, would come,
To the drowsy sound of the beetle's hum ;
Some, from the sweets of their flowery bed,
  Would start at the call with a glad surprise ;
And some would move with too nimble a tread,
  To shake the dew from the violet's eyes.
Some, from the tops of the moonlit trees ;
  Some, where the humming-bird's tiny nest,
Scarcely swayed in the fragrant breeze,
  As it stole from the prairies of the West ;
Some, on the back of the toad, would ride
  — For they loved all sorts of frolic and fun —
Some would step, with a stately pride ;
  Some would walk, and some would run ;
Some, on the wings of the Moth would fly ;
  Some would take the Fire-Fly's lamp,

And as it twinkled cheerily,
  Wend their way o'er Hill and Swamp ;
And giggle and laugh, as they strove to pass
Will-o'-the-Wisp, on his dark morass.
With Elfin fingers some would untwist
  The Morning-Glory's purple fold ;
And some would come, on the lowland mist,
  As it, chariot-like, before them rolled ;
And some, on the back of the Shooting-Star,
Would come to the trysting ground from far.
From Heaven above and Earth beneath ;
  From Hill and Vale and grassy Plain ;
From wheresoe'er God's creatures breathe,—
  They would come with might and main
    Members of the Elfin-Court ;
    And with Fairy glee and sport,
    Pass the moonlit hours away,
    Till the early dawn of day.

I I I.

But often, a Stream would cross their way ;
  And then, it was royal fun, to see
How the Nymphs and Water-Sprites obey
  A Law which bound them, loyally,
To keep their sacred precincts, free
From stranger-feet !   With roguish gleam,
You might see their elfin-faces beam,
Here and there, in the moonlit-stream,

As its ripples, merrily, danced along
To the sweet refrain of their gentle song.
But as soon as the Fays of the Land would cross
　To the other side, the Nymphs of the Stream
Would raise their tiny forms, and toss
　Their little waves ; and shout and scream,
With the myriad voices of Elfin spite ;
As they felt the thrill of a strange delight,
In seeking thus, to turn away,
The feet of the Intruding Fay.
They would call the Leech his blood to draw ;
　They would summon the Shrimp and Soldier-
　　Crab ;
They would bid the Pike, with his hungry maw,
　Follow him fast : and guide the stab,
Which the Sword-Fish, gave with his weapon grim,
As he sought to pierce the elfin-limb.
O ! but a weary time had they,
Who strove to win their toilsome way,
Across the Water-Sprites' domain :
But, when the other side, they gain,
They shout and sing, with elfin glee,
And haste to the place of their revelry.

IV.

It was a lovely spot to see !
　For the winds forgot their anger there ;
And they sighed, with so soft a melody,
　That, they scarcely, stirred the evening air !

And the stately trees their shadows threw,
Over against the sky of blue ;
As the moonbeams touched their tops with light,
Giving the shade a darker night,
Where the branches, arching overhead,
    A royal canopy upreared ;
And a carpet, soft as a Fairy's tread,
    Of grass, inlaid with flowers, appeared.
The little blue-eyed Forget-Me-Not,
Breathed its perfume round the spot ;
The graceful forms of the Maiden-Hair,
    Waved with a motion light and free :
As if it sought its life to share,
    With the fairy-leaved Anemone !
And the Daisy strove, with its cheerful face,
To lend fresh charm to the sacred place :
While Pansy, Asphodel and Rose,
All their loveliest tints disclose.
With mimic skill the Throne appeared,
On a base of pearly shells, upreared —
Phosphoric light, about it played :
    And wavy sprays of the Columbine
Let in the alternate light and shade,
    As its branches swayed in the soft moon-
    shine !
This was the Fay-King's Judgment-Seat.
And, ranged about in order meet,
    Above ; beneath ; on every hand,
With forms as light, and steps as fleet,

12

As a passing thought, around him stand,
The Little Ones of the Elfin-Land;
To execute the high decree,
Of this Fairy Court of Chivalry!

V.

Sometimes for revelry and sport,
The monarch would summon his fairy-court;
And throned on the Huleh Lily's crown,
In his royal state, look gayly down
On the myriad forms that thronged to pass,
    Out of brake and bush and flower;
Dancing merrily on the grass;
    Making love in the moonlit-bower;
In brilliant dress of state arrayed,
    Passing full before his view;
Glancing out of light and shade,
    Quick as thought, and bright as dew.
O! but his heart beat high with pride,
As, trooping round on every side,
His courtiers crowd with fun and glee,
To the chosen place of their revelry!
And as the Lily waved to and fro,
    To the gentle breath of the evening breeze;
He would smile to see them come and go,
    As they lead the dance 'neath the haunted trees!
His was as gorgeous a canopy,
As heart could wish or eye could see.

For the Lily's petals of snowy white
  Fringed with jewels the night had made,
Bent their arch of silvery light
  Over his head; and, in their shade,
Half-concealed and half-displayed,
  His roguish eyes, with a merry gleam,
The scene of their romp and sport, surveyed
  As it lay revealed in the bright moonbeam!

V I.

Sometimes, a fairy's heart would move,
With the tender thrill of human love.
They would own the glance of a maiden's eye;
And answer back her pensive sigh.
They would bask in the light of her gentle smile;
And make sweet sport with herself, the while.
And the elf-lock, with its cunning curl,
  On the brow where beauty lingers,
Told, how many a fair-haired girl,
  Felt the touch of fairy fingers!
Some, with the baby-oak, were born,
  As it burst the bonds of its acorn-cup;
And they came, with the dews of Night and Morn,
  To build its grand proportions up.
Through its years of early life;
Through its littleness and strife;
Through its growth of later years,
All their ministry appears.

And, when fully formed, it stood
Crowned, the Monarch of the Wood;
All its glory they would share;
Lift its branches high in air;
And join the swell of their sweet refrain,
To the whispering winds and the pattering rain!
O! but a merry time had they,
    Through the long, long life of the mountain-
        oak!
For they never grew old, and were just as gay
    Up to the last, when the woodman's stroke,
Its leafy honors took away,
    Or slow decay its substance broke.
Their lease of life together ran,
    For the Dryads shared the Oak-tree's state;
At the same point, their course began;
    At the same point, they met their fate.
The Tree fell, headlong, on the plain;
The Dryads never moved again!
Where no human eye can see,
    Gnomes their secret way pursue
Working always, silently,
    But with mischief, still in view.
Ever finding their delight,
In all little acts of spite.
Salamanders, in the fire,
    Sparkle with incessant glow:
Growing brighter still, as higher
    In the rising flames they go.

And as these their forms prolong,
  Deftly springing here and there:
Singing-Flames take up the song,
  Which they breathe upon the air!*
Rising up from Ocean's caves,
  Roguish water-sprites are seen;
Yielding, underneath the waves,
  Homage to their Virgin Queen!
Realms of beauty, rich and rare,
Yield them habitations there.
Brilliant forms of crystal spar,
Sparkling like the Northern Star,
Arch the high resounding domes,
Where they make their chosen homes.
Floors, where gems and pearls abound,
  Feel the tread of fairy-feet;
And the Coral groves resound,
  With their music, soft and sweet.
For Life is busy, beneath the wave;
  And forms of beauty meet us there,
In what we would call the Ocean *grave*,
  Richer than those of the upper air!
And this is my Story.   Don't you see,
  It comes as fresh as the Spring-time breeze,

* Is not the dream of Romance well-nigh ended? The *Popular Science Monthly* for April, 1873, has a notice in its *Miscellany*, of the *Practical Application of Singing-Flames*, by Dr. A. R. Irvine of the British Iron and Steel Institution!

12*

When it whispers its secrets, playfully,
  To the opening buds of the waving trees?"

VII.

"It's beautiful, Grandpa! But is it true?
I never saw such sprites — did you?"

"No, my Darling! I suppose,
That Nature no such creatures, knows.
But then, our race, in its early youth,
Blindly groping after the truth;
Knew little enough, of the God, whose power
Blazed in the Sun, and opened the Flower:
And so, in His place, they multiplied
  These fancied beings, with wondrous skill;
  And with power of working good or ill,
To almost any extent, supplied.
And yet, these dreams of wild romance,
Of fairy sport and fun and dance;
Can scarce, with the simple facts compare,
Which press on our notice everywhere.
The Rain comes down, on the thirsty ground
  In the gentle form of the Spring-time showers;
Or falls on the roof with a pattering sound;
  Or scarcely shakes the opening flowers.
But no little Fay was as cunning an Elf,
As each of its drops when seen by itself:

For it shone in the rays of the morning light,
With a beam, like that of the diamond, bright;
Or into the heart of the rose would steal;
    And, hiding away in silence there,
Would help its beauties to reveal
    And breathe its fragrance out on the air!
Or, it changed its form as the Sun rose high,
And mounted in vapor, to sail through the sky;.
And over the clouds in glory, threw
The delicate tints of the rainbow hue.
Or made the wintry landscape know
The treasures of the falling snow:
Or wreathed in many a strange device,
The crystal forms of the sparkling ice.

The Sun pours forth its beams of light;
But what is it, that makes those beams so bright?
Atoms of matter so small, that we,
Have no power their forms to see.
Spreading away through the thin, thin air;
    Filling all space, with their delicate motion;
Undulating everywhere;
    Light is the wave of this Fairy Ocean.
And the varied colors of things we see,
    Tell us how fast those wavelets move;
And how Little Things make harmony,
    In all around, beneath, above!
Ages ago, the sunbeams stole
    Into the heart of the growing tree;

And now, shut up in their beds of coal,
　They wait for their hour of liberty;
When — changing only their proper names —
Those beams come out, as frolicksome flames;
And up the chimney, dancing go,
While the house is filled with the pleasant glow;
Or they draw the train, as it speeds along,
Urged by the breath of the Sunbeam's Song!

Do you know, as the Ocean heaves its tide,
How its secret strength is all supplied?
Little Drops, beyond all number,
In its deep recesses slumber:
Ever moving to and fro,
Making up its ebb and flow;
Murmuring, in its low-voiced song;
　Thundering in the deaf'ning roar,
Which its swelling waves prolong,
　As they dash upon the shore!
O! the unseen power that dwells
　In the Little Things of Earth!
How impressively it tells
　Of the One who gave them birth!
Heaving in the storm-tossed main;
Waving in the ripening grain;
Sparkling in the sunbeam's light;
Glorying in the tempest's might;
Breathing perfume on the air;
Living, acting, everywhere,

Little Things their work pursue ;
Ever constant, ever new ;
Writing their Creator's Name,
    In the mountain-torrent's dash —
In the Lightning's livid flame ;
    In the Thunder's startling crash.
In the Snow-Flake ; in the Dew ;
And, in little toads, like you ! "

TWiLIGHT MUSINGS.

THERE are voices softly ringing,
   I shall hear on earth no more;
Tones of gentle music, singing
   To me from the Unknown Shore.

There are footfalls sounding near me,
   But they reach *my* ear alone;
Voices of the past which cheer me,
   With their old, familiar tone.

Forms that in the grave are lying
   Move around each path I tread.
They are living yet; for dying
   Does not leave us truly dead.

No! Our real Life surviveth
   Even in the act of death.
Resurrection but *reviveth*
   Germs of life that wait its breath.

I am richer for the union
   With the loved ones gone before ;
Longing more for the communion,
   Fuller Life shall yet restore !

May I not believe, that loved ones,
   Who, from earth have passed away,
Move, as angel forms about me ;
 • Ministering on my way?

When the twilight shadows darken ;
   Still, small voices on the air
Seem to make the spirit hearken
   For the Footstep on the stair !

Is it Memory that reminds me,
   Of Life's broken ties as such ?
Or the electric chain that binds me,
   Answering to some unknown touch ?

Powers of worlds unseen surround us ;
   Heaven is nearer than we think :
And the waves of Life around us,
   Fall, in murmurs, on its brink !

For, eternal things are lying
   Hidden by the spray and strife
Dashing round us, here ; and dying
   Is but birth to nobler life.

And its surges, sounding near us,
    Tell us of our Heavenly Home;
Whence, with dew-like thoughts to cheer us,
    Dwellers there oft round us come!

And they touch with unseen fingers,
    All the strings of inner life;
Waking many a thought which lingers,
    Sweetly, 'midst its din and strife.

When we pass beyond the River,
    We shall meet our loved ones there:
And the forms that most we've cherished,
    Shall be loved ones, as they were!

For we stand *outside* the Portal
    Of our Full Life's Blessedness:
When we enter in, Immortal,
    Shall our meed of joy be less?

THE STILL WATERS.

THERE is a Stream of which I drink,
   Whose Living Water flows
Softly, as on its mossy brink,
   The dew-drop, trembling, glows.

It does not flow from springs of earth;
   But, 'midst the Eternal Hills
On Sion's Mount, it has its birth,
   And sweetly, there distils.

And thence, pervadingly, it flows
   Through pastures green and fair;
Where Carmel's Vine, and Sharon's Rose
   Shed their best fragrance there.

And oft, the Saviour comes unseen,
   And with His sweetest smile,
Invites me to these pastures green,
   And bids me rest awhile.

How sweet, how heavenly is the place!
  For all around, above,
Tells of the riches of His grace,
  And whispers of His love.

And calm and still, the waters flow;
  And as I stoop to drink,
Bright gleams of heavenly radiance glow
  Upon the river's brink.

What are they? Shinings forth of grace;
  Bright foretastes from above,
Where Jesus shows unveiled His face;
  And feasts us with His love.

And gently as the evening dews
  Distil upon the flower:
The Living Water there, renews
  The fainting spirit's power.

Dear Saviour! only lead me there
  And I shall learn from Thee;
To walk amidst Earth's darkest care,
  From all distraction free!

THE CAPTIVE EAGLE.

AN Eagle, once condemned to be
Detained in long captivity;
At length was to be freed again.
The owner broke the captive's chain,
And waited near to see him rise,
And seek once more his native skies.
But no. He seems to heed it not:
   Listless, he treads the little round
That had, for years, described the spot
   That marked his chain's length on the ground.
And is it so? Is all forgot?
   Amid the ashes of Desire
That burned within him; is there not
   Some spark of the once glowing fire?
See! there's a kindling of his eye,
With one glance at his native sky.
One wing is partly stretched; and then
Is folded to his side again.
The other follows, at full length,
As if he questioned of its strength;

Then both, a moment opening wide,
Were quickly folded to his side.
But not for long. Some power, suppress'd,
Seems to be struggling in his breast.
Visions of distant fields of light,
Are rising dimly on his sight:
And voices of the far-off skies,
Seem to be calling him to rise.
Upward, one kindling glance he threw;
Close to his perch, his body drew;
Sprang forward, as in glad surprise,
And sought once more, his native skies.
One moment, round and round he flew,
In circles widening to his view;
One moment seemed to linger there,
Before he sought the upper air;
Then, mounting upward in his flight,
    As if all doubt, all fear was o'er;
Slowly he faded from the sight —
    The Captive Bird was free, once more!

Such is the Christian.   One, set free,
And called to use his liberty:
But oft, alas! he's called in vain.
For — like the Eagle, when his chain
At first was broken — knowing not,
    That faith in Jesus sets him free
From Sin's dominion ; on the spot
    Where he obtained his liberty,

He lingers, treading o'er and o'er
A round of duties, as before.
Unconscious of his freedom, he
Remains in dull captivity;
Careless of all that bids him rise,
And spread his pinions for the skies.
The sweet, pervading influence,
 That dew-like on the soul distils,
And wakens there, the new-born sense
 Of Sonship, as the spirit thrills
Beneath the Saviour's love; and we
Rise, in the perfect liberty,
Which love imparts, to comprehend
How, without measure, bound, or end,
That love exists for us; of this,
He knows not, nor conceives, the bliss.
How can he? Can the Eagle share
The keen delights of upper air,
While on his perch he, idly, sleeps?
And can the Christian, while he keeps
His place, within the broken chain
Of duties done, expect to gain
The consciousness of freedom? No.
Forth from such bondage he must go.
For, fields beyond the Eagle's flight,
 Invite his wing: and brighter skies
Than those illumed by earthly light,
 Call him persuasively to rise.

13 *

The Sense of Sonship, in the soul
   Seeks its own origin to prove;
And springing up from Law's control,
   Finds every law fulfilled in Love.
How high its flight! How wide its reach!
How deep, beyond the power of speech,
Its peace extends! How pure the air,
That floats around the spirit, there;
And, in its inspiration, brings
A feeling like a sense of wings,
Prompting the soul to rise and prove
The pure delights of perfect Love!

EPIGRAM.

*On hearing a friend of the Rev. —— complain of his
starving salary.*

I OWN it is hard: and I feel it afresh;
   Still, Candor the true reason owns.
If his people persist in refusing him flesh,
   It's because he *will* feed them with bones.

A PARABLE.

As the Sun looked out from the Eastern sky,
The Violet raised its deep-blue eye.;
And in soft and whispered accents said,
While the dew-drop bent its delicate head —
    This drop of dew,
    I have kept for you,
Through all the darkness of the night ;
Now, shine and make my dew-drop bright ;
    Bright for Thyself, O Sun !
And the Sunbeam entered the drop of dew, ·
Trembling there in the Violet blue ;
And it grew as bright as the costly gem,
That shines in the monarch's diadem !

The Morning passed ; and the drop of dew
Sparkled no more, in the eye of blue ;
For the Sunbeam kissed it all away.
Yet still, the Violet seemed to say,

151

I am not alone,
Though my dew-drop is gone:
For the fragrance it, lovingly wrought in me,
I yield as my best return to Thee;
For Thy grace to me, O Sun!
And the Sun smiled back, as he strove to lift
Up to himself the Violet's gift;
But, ere he could do it, the perfumed air
Told of its secret everywhere.

The Summer passed; and out of sight,
The Violet sank for the Winter's night.
But the Autumn leaves above its head,
Rustling to the wild wind's tread,
Heard her words, as she softly said,
Though I'm out of sight,
For the Winter's night,
Thou wilt bring me forth again to the light;
And again, Thou wilt make my dew-drop bright,
Bright for Thyself, O Sun!
I will bring thee forth, the Sun replied,
As the Violet bowed her head and died;
And the South Wind for her burial sighed.

INSCRIPTION ON A SUN-DIAL.

Non numero horas nisi serenas.

A DIAL, bearing this device
　　Attracts the traveller's view:
Teaching in sounding phrase, a thought, ·
　　More specious far than true:
I number not the passing hours,
　　Unless the sun be shining: —
Forgetting, that Life's loveliest flowers,
　　Are in the shade reclining.

A Day is born.　But when the Night
　　Has closed its little round:
We find, that hours both dark and bright,
　　Have joined to mark its round.
And Life records its total sum,
　　Not by the bright hours only;
But by rehearsing all that 's done
　　In times both bright and lonely.

The sweetest flowers are never, those
　　Beneath a cloudless sky:

The Lily, Violet and Rose,
  Would wither there and die.
And all Life's loveliest graces are
  By the same Law unfolded ;
And yield their richest fragrance, where
  'Neath shady skies they 're moulded.

The Diamond flashes in the light,
  And yields a softer ray ;
E'en when the darkness of the night
  Has quite shut out the day.
But yet, the brilliant gem had birth
  Not where the sunbeam found it ;
But in the gloomy caves of earth,
  With deepest night around it.

The Pearl, before the noonday light
  Displays its loveliest hue :
But 't was in darkness and in night,
  Its glorious beauties grew.
For, by a process none can tell,
  All sun, all light excluded ;
Its birthplace is the oyster's shell,
  By slow degrees exuded.

To the warm sunshine's genial ray,
  Each flower-bud makes reply ;
And gives its hue and fragrance way,
  Beneath the summer-sky.

But yet, those hidden secrets were
  Within the bud preparing;
And cloudy skies and sunny hours,
  Are but its work declaring.

The Day has glories of the Light
  Oft seen yet ever new;
But grander still are those which Night
  Discloses to our view;
And while Life oft, seems out of tune,
  We'll reverently remember,
The Year that brings us flowers in June,
  Has frost for its December.

Our Life has many a summer sky,
  On which no cloud appears;
And Hope shines bright in many an eye,
  That ne'er was wet with tears.
But, when we would its sum disclose,
  And its attainments single;
We find its grandest deeds are those
  Where Clouds and Sunshine mingle.

We will not murmur then; nor wish
  Our sky was always bright:
But number still, Life's varied hours,
  Though some are in the night.
And, let us ne'er this truth forget,
  Nor yield to hopeless sorrow:
That though to-day our Sun be set,
  'T will rise again to-morrow!

THE WHITE STONE.

" To him that overcometh, will I give . . . . . a white stone, and in the stone a new name written, which no man knoweth, saving he that receiveth it."

EACH man has his own history, formed and moulded,
    As are the Spring-time leaves,
Within the autumn buds; and thence, unfolded,
    By powers he scarce perceives.

That history is unwritten.   None can render
    Its workings into speech;
Or tell, how far in all that's deep or tender,
    The chords of Nature reach.

But deep within, we feel their low vibrations,
    Each for himself alone;
And thrill beneath the touch of aspirations,
    By others all unknown.

God hears their silent workings: for He readeth
    Each thought of every soul:
And gives Himself, as every one most needeth
    In fulness for the whole.

He still is One ; but in His benedictions,
    Is not the same to all.
He suits Himself to each, with such restrictions,
    As answer to their call.

All flowers live in the Sun ; and each appealeth,
    For its own special hue :
And each, in its full beauty, but revealeth,
    What, from His beams, it drew.

In light, in heat, and in full rainbow-splendors,
    Those beams around it play ;
But each receiveth, only what it renders,
    Back to the Eye of Day !

It comprehends no more ; and its appealing
    Is for that hue alone.
And Leaf, Bud, Petal are alike revealing,
    How each the light has known.

And thus, all creatures have in God, their being ;
    Each in His fulness lives.
But not alike, are we His glories seeing,
    And not alike He gives.

You may not read what God, to me, is showing
    When I His fulness prove ;
Nor may another drink the stream, whose flowing
    To you bears Light and Love.

The new name hath its secrets ; which he knoweth
    To whom that name is given :

14

And to that secret each believer groweth,
   And in it finds his heaven.

His *unexpanded* heaven, whose full unfolding
   His future Life shall be;
And here, his spirit, blossom-like, is moulding,
   Into its symmetry.

For each one *is* his name; and comprehendeth,
   Not all that Jesus is;
But what a kindred nature apprehendeth,
   By making truly his.

That name is but the measure of the union,
   We have with Jesus' love;
The rich foretasting of that sweet communion,
   Awaiting us above!

God calls us by it; and its meaning rises,
   Upon the spirit's sight
In gradual unfolding; and surprises
   With strange, new-born, delight.

For we perceive that meaning, to our measure
   Of victory over sin;
And all beyond, is but an unknown treasure,
   Lying concealed within.

O! for the peace that comes from this revealing;
   When, quivering through the frame,
The soul in its deep consciousness is feeling,
   The secret of its name!

FELLOWSHIP.

THERE is a Harp of countless strings
In Nature's works around us;
And rich the music that it brings,
When earthly cares surround us.
Its sweetest tones may peal around,
Unheard by outward senses;
But reach us, in the calm profound
Of dew-like influences.

There's music in the rustling trees,
And in the sky-lark's soaring;
Sweet music in the evening breeze,
And in the Ocean's roaring.
There's music in the varied tones
Of animals that love us;
Grand music in the solemn march
Of suns and stars, above us.

The Daisy lifts its dew-lit eyes,
In Nature's deep communing;
To the sweet light of far-off skies,
Its inward.growth attuning.

Millions of miles those sunbeams came,
  Their light with all things sharing;
Yet life and strength and healthful growth.
  To this frail floweret bearing.

So, we too, stand 'mid countless powers,
  Whose influences surround us;
And waken thoughts, like summer flowers,
  Above, beneath, around us.
From every object round us, we
  New impulses may borrow;
And answer back the minstrelsy,
  Of Nature's joy and sorrow.

There's music, sweeter far than this:
  Though this is near the portals
Of something like the sweetest bliss,
  That God has given to mortals.
Yet, 't is the *portals* only; and
  We must the building enter;
Ere we can hear the solemn, grand,
  Rich, music of the centre.

It comes, in tones of sympathy
  For all, our nature sharing;
And claims an interest, large and free,
  In every want they 're sharing.
It 's not in nation; not in race;
  It 's not in outward station.

It's founded solely, on the place,
God gave it in Creation.

We read it there; and own the claim
He meant it to engender;
And, for the love of His dear Name,
Whate'er it calls for, render.
It is the pulse of the "one blood,"
Our common nature filling;
The under-tones of brotherhood,
With low, deep music thrilling.

We move among the mighty dead,
Who long have gone before us;
And seem to feel the silent tread
Of ages passing o'er us.
We think their thoughts; their hopes renew;
Revive their aspirations;
And feel our pulses thrill anew,
With their best inspirations.

There's yet a purer joy than this.
'T is in the soul upspringing,
Like waters in the wilderness,
Or birds, in deserts, singing.
A Peace and Joy which freely flow,
E'en when we're tempest-driven;
But which *they* only, come to know,
Whose fellowship's in Heaven.

14 * L

It is the spirit's full accord
　　With all that God has spoken:
The harmony of thought and word,
　　By no one discord broken.
Not that his reason comprehends;
　　But that his heart approveth;
And the best reason meets and blends,
　　In him who truly loveth.

There may not be an utterance heard,
　　To mark the soul-communing;
But O! its deepest depths are stirred,
　　As harp-strings are, in tuning.
And thence, in musical accord,
　　Its varied powers are waking;
And, with sweet music to the Lord,
　　Its melody is making.

The Lamp, that burns with perfumed oil,
　　Sheds sweetest light around it;
And Faith is brightest, while the toil
　　And cares of Life surround it.
For, deep within the soul, the light,
　　Of heavenly truth is burning;
And songs are sweetest when the night
　　Of Grief, to Joy is turning.

THE DEAD CHRIST.*

THE work of Death, at last, is done,
  And Jesus sleeps, in calm repose:
The circle of His life is run,
  In seeming triumph for His foes.
He sleeps in death, who came to prove
The fulness of eternal love.

Approach. And, as you venture near,
  To gaze with reverence on the dead,
Tread softly; for the Sleeper here,
  Seems to be resting on His bed.
You scarce can think, repose so deep,
Can be aught else than healthful sleep.

A veil is gently o'er Him thrown;
  So gently, that you seem to see
Through it; and, on the sculptured stone,
  To trace the spotless purity,

* The veiled Statue of The Dead Christ, in the family chapel
of *S. Maria della Pieta de Sangri*, Naples, is a work of wonderful power. Indeed, there is no piece of statuary in the
city, that can be justly compared with it.

That, halo-like, shone round His head,
And lingers sweetly o'er the Dead.

The Crown of Thorns lies by His feet;
 The Hammer and the Nails are there;
The instruments of Death, complete,
 The story of the Cross declare.
His wounded hands and feet and side,
Repeat to us how Jesus died.

Of His mysterious agony
 There rests no trace upon His brow
In glorious tranquillity,
 The Dead Christ sleeps before you now;
You see the lines in form and face,
That Death alone has power to trace.

Yes, Death; but something more. Alone,
 Death could not cause what, here, you see.
The sculptor's art has made the stone
 Speak to us of the mystery
Of Him who thus in death could lie,
And yet, in death do more than die.

Do *more?* Yes. Had He not full power
 Over His life, to hold it still
Against all foes; or at the hour,
 To lay it down of His own will?

And this high purpose seems to speak,
From His calm brow and pallid cheek.

He seemed a victim. Was He? No!
    For Jesus *acted* in His death :
He gave His Spirit leave to go ;
    And willed His own departing breath.
Christ was not passive when He died :
The Conqueror was The Crucified !

You gaze ; and feel the sculptor's art
    Throw its strong spell upon the soul :
Till, captive both in mind and heart,
    You yield yourself to its control
And feel — for words, here, ask no breath —
This, this is Jesus in His death !

All-conquering Saviour ! In the light
    Of this Thy wondrous love to me ;
Earth's shadows grow divinely bright,
    And love blooms into liberty.
Sin cannot reign within the soul,
That lives within Thy strong control.

I gaze, in awe and wonder, till
    The great conception fires my soul :
And wakes, with its electric thrill,
    A deathless love, whose strong control
Brings every thought, with sweet accord,
To wait in service, on its Lord.

AN AUTUMN RAMBLE.

IT was a day
Of Autumn's choicest beauty. The fair Earth
Lay like a garden, in the smile of Heaven.
The sky was cloudless: and September's sun
Looked forth, in gentle gladness, as its beams
Danced on the ripples of the murmuring stream;
Or wooed the wild-bee from its home, to sip
The sweets, that lingered in the fading flowers.
The wind scarce swayed the clover's leaf, or shook
The dew-drops from the fern; yet bush and brake
Dropped, silently, their sere leaves to the ground.
The flocks and herds had cropped their morning
    meal,
And sought repose beneath the spreading trees.
The wild birds carolled gayly in the woods;
And the deep calm of purity and peace,
Investing Nature like an atmosphere,
Broke on the troubled passions of the soul,
Like the first sunbeam through the parting clouds.

I had been musing on the Life of Man,
The history of Nations, and the end,

Which, in the cycle of revolving years,
Returns alike for both ; and I went forth
To hold communion in the woodland shade,
With the deep mysteries of the Universe,
To draw instruction from the falling leaf,
The change of seasons, and the flight of time !
There is an eloquence in Nature's voice,
Whene'er we list her teachings. She may speak,
In the soft zephyr of the Summer's eve ;
Thunder in Tempests ; murmur in the breeze ;
Or woo us, in her gentlest tones, to read
The lessons she inscribes on all her works.
And thus, she meets us, in the deep, calm, wood ;
And in its stillness, finds a voice, which speaks
Of the Eternity of Change, which seems
The Vital Spirit of the Universe.
I wandered on, in silence ; and the scene
Grew eloquent in wisdom. At my feet,
The grasshopper chirped forth its morning song ;
Rejoicing in the consciousness of life,
Even in the season that insured its doom.
The butterfly flew onward in my path ;
And paused a moment, on the withered leaves ;
The beauteous Emblem of Immortal Life,
Reposing on the subjects of decay.
Beside me lay a fallen Tree, which once,
Lifted its branches 'mid the noblest there ;
Perhaps had towered above them ; for it spoke

E'en in its present overthrow, of strength
Superior to its fellows. But the axe
Had brought its leafy honors to the ground.
Its leaves had mingled with the earth, which gave
Their texture and their beauty. One by one,
The hand of Time had torn its limbs away,
And 'reft it of its substance; which became
A portion of the sod on which it lay,
And blossomed in the wild flower by its side.
Life, leaf, limb, substance, all were gone; but yet,
Its form remained as witness of the past.
Its *form* alone; the traveller's gentlest touch
Might crush it to the dust. But there it lay,
Lifeless and withered; yet the source of life,
To much that grew around it, and to all
That grew upon it; for the lapse of time
Had called fresh beauties from its withered trunk;
New forms of life adorned it. Rich, green moss
Enclosed it, like a vestment. Fair, young flowers
Too slight, e'en for the dew-drop's weight, came
        forth,
And, in their delicate beauty, seemed to smile,
That Life could triumph by its own decay.

And such is Human Destiny. The fate
Of all that live, is figured in that tree.
The countless members of the Human Race,
Spring into being; act their part, and die.

But Time renews them. From their ashes spring
Beings of other mould ; and that which they
Had taken from the general mass of life,
They pay again, when they bequeath their dust,
To nourish other beings, who in turn,
Even in their dissolution, still become
Fountains of active life. And thus the wheel
Of Destiny rolls onward ; and men die,
Yet live in those who follow them, and make
A portion of the Future as the Past.
The nations of past ages are no more ;
Or live, in the remembrance of those minds
Which made their names immortal and shall bear
Their fame and glory through all coming time.
Their roots struck deeply, and their branches
     spread,
And shadowed other nations ; yet they fell,
Like a Colossus, by the hand of Time
In the vast Sea of Being. Where they stood
Others have risen, nourished by their strength ;
And, like those flowerets, on that withered trunk,
Attained their life, amid decay and death.

And is this all ?   Is there no hope beyond ?
Is man to be resolved in such a doom ?
Shall we collect a handful of his dust ;
And scattering it upon the breeze, exclaim
This much remains — no more !

15

No more, indeed,
We read on Nature's page. But there's a Voice
That whispers to us — "Man shall never die.
I am the Resurrection and the Life!"
And they who sleep in Him, shall live again
In blessedness, that knows of no decay;
And Nature shall put on her Spring-time robes;
And Autumn's breath shall scatter them no more!

"THOU SETTEST ME BEFORE THY FACE
FOREVER."

AND is it so ?   Amidst the blaze
　Of all the countless worlds I see ;
O ! does my Heavenly Father's gaze
　Turn with a glance of love to me ?
Yes ; in His Word these lines I trace —
"Thou settest me before Thy Face ! "

"*Thou* settest me."   And who shall dare,
　Remove me from that glorious place ?
Or from my state of favor there,
　Conceal the smilings of Thy face ?
Thy hand hath set me ; and until
Some stronger hand, some mightier will
Than Thine is found, I shall abide,
Secure whatever may betide !

"Thou *settest* me " — not for an hour,
　Or peradventure to remain ;
But, by Thy love's constraining power,
　That place forever to maintain.

Unchangeably Thy people prove
Thy sovereign and eternal love;
And, by the triumphs of Thy grace,
Forever dwell before Thy face!

"Thou settest *me*" — Almighty Lord!
It needs such records of Thy word;
Such plain, undoubted truths to prove,
This triumph of Thy sovereign love!
"*Me*" — in each moment of my life;
Each scene of triumph and of strife;
"*Me*" — in each sorrow, joy or care
Thy love appoints my soul to bear;
Alike, if joy's ecstatic thrill
Or sorrow's pang my bosom fill:
In every scene whate'er it be,
    I read the record of Thy grace;
    In Life; In Death; Eternally —
      "*Thou settest me before Thy Face!*"

TO A FRIEND ON HIS ORDINATION.

You've gained the end, My Youthful Friend,
    Which long, you've been pursuing;
And now, before you further go,
    Let us your path be viewing.
Its points and bearings let us trace;
    Where lies each special danger;
That, when it comes indeed, the case
    May be to you, no stranger.

O! 'tis a glorious work, on which
    You now are called to enter;
A work, on which each thought and wish
    And plan in life should centre.
There is no work so grand, if you
    But rightfully pursue it;
Nor aught that works so false a life
    For those who wrongly view it.

Therefore be honest with thyself;
    And now, that you've attained it,

Seek only how you may promote
   His glory who ordained it.
Be true to *that*, as Paul was true,
   With high and pure devotion;
And keep your little self from view,
   Nor heed its slightest motion.

All canting phrase and pious talk,
   Hold in deep detestation :
Remembering, 't is your daily walk,
   That speaks your vindication.
'T is what *you are* that ends the strife
   About the truth, you 're preaching :
And men will heed a Christ-like life
   That spurn all other preaching.

Exact not from your fellow-men,
   The Shibboleth of party;
But let *all* truth find you its friend;
   Open, sincere and hearty.
Whate'er it calls for, freely speak;
   And calmly stand beside it :
Truth's resurrection-power will seek
   A place where none can hide it.

Seek not to gain the foremost place;
   But take the lowliest station,
Where you may do the Master's work,
   And gain His approbation.

I serve, is nobler than *I rule*,
  Though men may not believe it;
And they stand first in Jesus' school,
  Who lovingly receive it.

On *service* then, not power or place,
  Is true distinction founded;
And all the best rewards of grace,
  By labors, most, are bounded;
Perhaps on Life's most active fields;
  Perhaps of calm endurance;
Wherever placed, Grace always yields
  This fruit of its assurance.

O! do not think success in Life,
  By outward marks decided.
He gains it most, who, in the strife,
  By Truth alone is guided.
Would you succeed?   The winner's place,
  By righteous judgment warded;
Will be for him, who runs the race,
  By Faith and Patience guarded!

The crown at last decks many a brow,
  Who dreams not what he's wearing;
And they are oft the lowliest, now
  Who noblest gifts are sharing.
But Pride so mingles with the race,
  Where, least, you think to find it;

That Self-Assertion wins the place,
  While Merit lags behind it.

No human hand can hold the scales,
  That character is weighed in ;
And oft, the feeling most prevails,
  That least we make parade in.
Therefore let Truth and Justice lead ;
  Put Jesus in the centre ;
And let no thought go out in deed,
  But what through Him may enter.

The Bishop's office you 'll revere ;
  But seek not to attain it.
For lofty station few can bear,
  E'en when they rightly gain it.
The Mitre and the Crown of Thorns,
  Are scarce one spirit sharing ;
And he whose brow the first adorns,
  Not oft, the last is wearing.

All honor to their glorious names,
  Who, in this lofty station,
Made life, in every deed, proclaim
  A true soul's vindication !
White; Griswold; Potter; Johns and Meade;
  —Thank God! that we have known such !
Thrice blest, if in our hour of need,
  We shall again be shown such !

Whate'er it costs, preach thou the Word,
    As governed by the preaching ;
And hearts shall, everywhere, be stirred,
    Responsive to the teaching.
Preach ; as a man that truly, knows
    The Gospel's inspiration.
Preach ; as a man whose spirit glows,
    With Christ and His Salvation.

O ! 'tis in grand and stirring times,
    The Master bids you serve Him :
And he, who now would do His work,
    To earnest toil must nerve him.
Therefore be strong : for duties wait.
    Be calm : for they may try thee.
And the Lord whose work you do, will still,
    With strength for each supply thee !

Stand ; where the old Reformers stood;
    Nor fear to take their station.
The Cause for which *they* shed their blood,
    May need thy attestation.
Stand for the Truth; and when He comes,
    Whose standard thou art bearing :
As thou hast borne the Cross, thou shalt
    A Crown of Life be wearing !

M

THE VISION OF LOVE.

Delivered before the Society of the Sons of St. George, at their Centennial Anniversary, April 23, 1872.

I FELL asleep, the other day:
   — At least I did to outward seeming —
And while I thus, unconscious lay,
   By some strange chance I fell to dreaming;
And as to form my visions grew,
They took the following shape and hue:

It is said when the World was just fresh in the smile
   Of its youthful existence, tho' blooming and fair,
It reposed in the light of its Maker the while,
   Young Love had not smiled yet, and sadness
      was there.
When lo! from the Ocean, one bright, sunny day,
   A vision of Glory arose on the sight:
It burst forth from the waves, in their turbulent play,
   And shed round them the splendor of beauty and
      light.

O ! fair was her form as it floated along ;
  And brightly the rainbow glanced forth from the
    spray ;
And the waves seemed to murmur an eloquent song
  As they fell 'neath her footsteps and vanished
    away.
Hope tended her pathway, and Peace followed
    near
. There was Joy all around her and Glory above ;
And the eye that beheld her, though dimmed with
    a tear,
  Grew bright 'neath the glance of the Goddess
    of Love !

And thus from the waves of the Ocean of Life,
  Love rises in beauty and gladness, to throw
Her charm o'er the waters of sorrow and strife
  And spread o'er their darkness her beautiful
    Bow.
The sorrows that darken ; the passions that blight ;
  Each hope and each feeling, all yield to her sway ;
And the brow that would else, have been shrouded
    in night,
  Is bright with the radiance that beams on her way !

Such was my dream. And as I woke,
  With sudden start, the spell that bound me,
At once, like some fair mirror broke,
  And left its shining fragments round me.

But on their surface, I could trace
  Glimpses of truth, so brightly shining,
That they may fitly, claim a place,
  In this, the wreath that here I'm twining,
For the bright memories, which to-day,
In every bosom move and play!
And what would life be, were it not
  For the strange Instinct, from above;
Which, from the waves of every lot,
  Calls forth the radiant form of Love?
Love of our Country! How, to-day
  In every heart its fires are burning!
How to that dear Land, far away,
  Our fondest thoughts and prayers are turn-
    ing!
How Memory, with its magic touch,
Revives the scenes we love so much;
And brings before the spirit's view,
What only spirit can renew.
Our Father's House — the home where we
Passed the bright days of Infancy —
We see it yet, in all the glow,
Which Childhood's recollections throw
Around the much-loved spot. Again
We live the life that charmed us then;
Thrill with our Childhood's hopes and fears;
Weep, once again, our Childhood's tears;
Our School-boy mischief, all renew;
And share the fun, and — *thrashings*, too!

Once more, around our Mother's knee,
— God's best and earliest Temple, — we
Kneel, with clasped hands and reverent air,
To say, once more, our Childhood's prayer.
Alas ! that from Life's later day,
Those words, so much, should pass away !
Land of our Fathers ! still to Thee,
   Though the wide Ocean rolls between,
Our love holds fast its loyalty
   And keeps Thy memory in us green !
We love to think upon Thy name ;
And feel, that, on the Scroll of Fame,
There 's none that takes a loftier place,
Or wears it with a nobler grace !
Great, in Thy power for good or ill ;
Great, in Thy Sons' exhaustless skill ;
Great, in the energies of will,
That, from Thy little Island Throne,
Circles the earth ; and in each zone,
Records some deed of greatness, done
To testify, before the Sun,
Of England's influence, spreading o'er
The World's wide bounds, from Shore to Shore !
What if the Sun does never set
   Upon Thy wide dominions ; we
Deem it a nobler triumph, yet,
   That the first Torch of Liberty,
Was lighted on Thy shores.   We read
Of the brave bands of Runny-Mead,

16

Who wrung from John's unwilling hand
The *Magna Charta* of our Land ;
And own the honest pride that claims
Kindred with these time-honored names !
Hampton and Sydney too, are Thine —
   And Milton, Chatham, Shakespeare, Thou
May'st in one wreath of glory, twine
   And wear the garland on Thy brow !
We share the pride ; the glory, share,
Of all the honors Thou dost bear ;
And, with exulting bosoms, claim
Oneness with Thine all-honored Name !
Yet, while as England's sons, to Thee
We offer thus, our loyalty ;
In the same act, we bring to view,
The Land of our Adoption, too.
Thee too we love !   Thee too we claim
As kindred of one common name :
Rejoice in all that proves Thee great,
In Arts and Arms ; in power and state ;
And shows Thee, standing side by side,
With England, in her noblest pride !
Long may Thy glorious Banner wave
   Its ample folds o'er Land and Sea !
We'll, only, ask to dig the Grave,
   Of every thought of Jealousy
Between two kindred Powers, whose pride,
Whose noblest pride, should be to stand
Shoulder to shoulder ; hand to hand ;

In waging still, that grandest fight,
For God, for Freedom, and the Right
In which, nought ever should divide
    Our Native and Adopted Land !
We 'll take Old England's Flag and Thine,
    And weaving their broad folds together :
We 'll only ask that they may twine,
    In sunny and in stormy weather,
As peacefully as now, they blend
In loving converse, to the end !,
And should their folds be blown aside,
By passion, prejudice or pride :
We 'll hope — and this is all we want —
That Little Vic. and General Grant,
As Queen and President may stand,
    And, 'changing speech across the water ;
Say, as they clasp each other's hand,
    Peace 'twixt the Mother and the Daughter !

Nor is this all.   In its embrace,
    Love is not to *one* Land confined :
But, circling o'er the Earth's wide space,
    Takes in the whole of human kind.
For Man, *as man*, its bosom thrills ;
For Man, as man, its measure fills ;
Man, made in God's own image ; Man,
Encircled by the Eternal Plan,
Which seeks to bring a rebel race,
Redeemed, before the Father's face ;

This is its measure ; running o'er
    With love to all, when, from His place
Within — as Life's controlling power —
    God moves, effulgent, in His grace.
All love is His !   Of Country : Kind :
    Or Individual : all proceeds,
From His one, over-ruling Mind,
    And fills up all our human needs !
He is its Central Sun ; and we
Move in our sphere, harmoniously,
Just as we learn to meet each claim
For help, for love, in His dear Name !

Sons of St. George !   We are here,
    To tell again Life's oft-told tale :
To yield the smile : to drop the tear,
    As Memory slowly, lifts the veil
That hides the buried past from view.
What recollections here renew
Their hold upon us !   How they sweep
Like waves, across the swelling deep ;
Rising and falling, as we thrill,
With thoughts that now, our bosoms fill !
One Hundred years ago, and we
Had birth, as a Society !
And yet, to-day no mark appears,
To tell us of advancing years.
No faltering step : no trembling hand
Proclaims the weakness of our Band ;

But stronger, heartier, than before,
  We trust our vigor to renew;
And bring again the days of yore,
  When Childhood, in a century, grew
To its dimensions; and the dew
Of Youth was sparkling on his frame,
Who, half a thousand years, could claim!
So *we* would trust: and in this hope,
Draw out St. George's horoscope!
Let rolling years Thy strength renew!
Its wisdom and its vigor, too
Let Time impart!   Let every year
  Mould Spring-time blossoms for the next;
And when *they*, in their bloom, appear
  — As thoughts included in the Text —
Let no untimely frosts destroy
The promise of the Autumn's joy!
Thus, still, in union let us stand:
Clasping — as one united band —
Our Native and Adopted Land!

16 *

THE SECRET.

"The secret of the Lord is with them that fear Him."

Father! it is not what I think,
   That is always best for me:
For dangers hover near the brink
   Of the fancied good I see.
But I would, with cheerful spirit, drink
   The cup that pleaseth Thee.

I know that clouds will often, shade
   The paths o'er which I go:
But I walk in peace; for they always lead
   Where the living waters flow;
And the fragrant plant is often, made
   'Neath shady skies to grow.

I do not fear the toil or strife
   Of witnessing for Thee:
For there's a spring of quenchless life,
   Thou hast opened up for me;
And I know the bliss Thy children feel,
   When the Truth has made them free.

If Grief should come with heavy tread,
  Or Joy with radiant air;
The Lord, on whom I wait, has said
  He will every burden bear;
And the Saviour's smile in the worst estate,
  Makes sunshine everywhere.

So, I ask Thee, Father, for the rest,
  The *spirit* rest, that flows
From leaning on the Saviour's breast
  In calm and sweet repose:
That questions not, but owns as best,
  Whate'er Thy hand bestows!

I have a part in Thee to claim,
  Which others may not know:
The secret of that hidden name
  Which Thou alone, canst show:
That tells me what to Thee I am,
  And sweetly *makes* me so.

I do not all its fulness know;
  But the way o'er which I move
Has streams of blessedness that flow
  From this Fountain of Thy Love.
And while I wait in peace below
  He guards me from above!

And thus, I gain the perfect peace,
  That Faith alone can bring;

Learn from my own vain work to cease
  And in the desert sing;
Making sweet music in the heart
  If *He* but touch its strings.

Therefore, if now Thou askest me,
  What most dost thou desire ?
I would my answer still might be,
  What Thou seest I most require:
There is no lowlier wish than this
  And I could not breathe a higher!